Collective Humanity

An LGBTQ+ Anthology of Imaginative Fiction and Poetry

Collective Tales Publishing

Collective Humanity
An LGBTQ+ Anthology of Imaginative Fiction and Poetry

In Memory of Trixie Bloom
1966-2022

Contents

Introduction

Collective Humanity: An LGBTQ+ Anthology is all about metamorphis. We feature stories about transformation, about understanding differences, rewriting history, about becoming our best selves.

The stories and poems in this anthology capture many different interpretations of what it means to transform, grow, and become. We hope you enjoy each and every unique vision.

By purchasing this book, you're not just supporting queer authors and allies by reading their work and hearing their stories, you're also supporting the community.

We started this project because we wanted to give back to the local LGBTQ+ community. We will be donating our net profits from the sales of the anthology to queer-serving charities and nonprofits in Utah, such as the Utah Pride Center.

Thank you to everyone who shared their stories and made this book happen. Together, we're showing that everyone's story matters.

Thanks for being part of the magic!

Overthrown

Ginevra Mancinelli

To be good at killing, you can't be afraid of dying. That's what my grandfather always told me, and he'd heard it from his father, who'd heard it from his, and so on. They said it all came from one legendary warrior of our family centuries ago. A general among generals. Someone who'd died taking down everyone else.

To be honest, I don't even know why I'm thinking of this right now. Iros'm sitting on top of this pile of charred corpses, my father's old sword in my left hand, and these soulless bodies are wearing plates that bear the crest of our house—the maw of this legendary, gigantic beast two snouts and too many horns to sound real, but still plagued our lands at some point. For once, I'm not even the one responsible for the massacre. As my adoptive brother would say, I was late to the party.

It sucks because I know Father will blame me again, and the last time he did, I got myself a scar that traces down my ribs and dips between the small of my back. The Count of Ghostfort is a man who believes in fair trials and fair duels, and I'd simply lost against him.

Though I'm not sure how a duel's fair if one must fight against their teacher.

I hop down the foul pile, feeling somewhat rested after that face-planting of mine down the hill to reach the battlefield, and take two long strides toward the abandoned pillar at the center of my hometown, Ghostfort. The pillar's nothing but a tall spike with a sealed door facing east, and I don't even know why the people who built it bothered carving an entrance; the pillar looks so narrow that only a child, or a tiny human, could have entered it. I'm sure there's a good explanation and some mysterious tale behind this pillar, but I never really paid attention when I still attended the atheneum in the capital. I'm not good at history, and I'm certainly not interested in religious folklore to care if they really walled a woman up in there. As everyone else before me in the Beausoleil family, I'm only good at one thing. Killing.

It sounds cliché, even in my head; it reminds me of one of those plays at the opera, in the capital, where my brother Florent would drag me every first dusk day of the month. The ladies in those plays always fainted at the same moment, when the story culminated with a massive, gore-filled battle, and a ranged warrior on a horse would come in to save the day. It's never earned and very much predictable, and that's how I feel at this moment.

I bend to grab a handful of dirt and ashes at the base of the pillar to bless the blade I hold. Again, I am not sure I'm doing this correctly, but if it brings me luck, like the temple maidens claim, I won't turn it down.

The blade feels heavier and my shoulders slump a bit; maybe I'm a little frightened. Who wouldn't be, if they were about to sneak inside a palace—a fortress—to chop the Great General's head? Right now, I have little to no choice. The scrawny man shipped Florent to the islands of the Far East, to the Enclave, and he's taken down every noble house that remained in this northern part of the continent so that the top positions in the Great General's council would pass on to women and men of his choosing. He's got alchemists, and some say even magic to help him see what others can't, which is why I stole my father's old sword. I remember him saying this one, with the gray and black hues, repels that kind of magic.

If it turns out it was just another legend... Let's not go there.

I scratch away an itch on the inside of my wrist and promptly cover the exposed brown skin by tugging on my crimson sleeve.

So, maybe there's another reason I want to take down the ugly man with a nose that always reminded me of a bird's beak, but thinking too much about it could be dangerous. Saggy Throat sent me on a fake mission that lasted months, in the continent across the Southern Bay, where I almost died in a massive explosion alongside a group tasked to dig out precious jewels and ritual items. I'd been having fun till then; I met a woman at the Bridge Tavern, the type of woman who gets to annoy you so fast you forget your name or how to spell simple words to update your family on the mission progression. She said her name was Lena, but I never got to know if she spoke the truth; there wasn't much talking involved when she straddled my legs or pressed her curls against mine at night.

Either way, and as much as I'd like to know how Lena fared across the bay, I have to end the madness that's about to raze my hometown.

I try not to feel too much as I drag my heels into the muddy snow and in the castle's direction. My straight black hair slaps against my face and the long strands flap in the wind like a worn banner, and the cold bites at my face. It makes my eyes watery, and I narrow the almond-shaped orbs I inherited from another grandparent I never met.

When I think about it, I never spend time around my family, save for Florent. I run my palm over my round, soft nose, and keep marching. Winter isn't my season, but this could be my last winter.

I don't expect the Great General to have no guards ready to fight back. The scouts I graciously questioned in the woods earlier said most troops rode west, and even when I cut off one scout's hand, they'd insisted few men remained at the fortress.

It's suspicious, and I hope the funny ash from the pillar blessed me enough to parry whatever blood magic the Great General could be ready to use.

My silhouette blends in the surrounding shadows, and my free hand checks the hilts of the sister blades on my back. I stole those too from Father's armory, but is it stealing if your old papa's been missing for months? For all I know, the Great General could've gotten his hands on him, just like the other noblemen who control sections of Ghostfort. The lighter swords are in place, and I have a pouch of smoke powder resting against my right hip—in case I must face more guards than expected.

I'm not endurant. I'm not the type of fighter who would last on the battlefield. I'm not ashamed of that; everyone has their own specialty.

With the two short towers hugging the core of this place that smells like eroded stone and lost most of its defined angles, the Duke's Fort reminds me of an old man's hunched figure as I stand next to the water mill, the lulling sound of the river doing nothing to quell the urgency in my bones. Part of me wonders why the Great General didn't rename the fort after the Duke of Ghostfort passed away six moons ago, seeing how he plainly took control of everything. But I'm stalling here, the useless thoughts swimming in my mind, trying to distract me from the reality that I could die within the next hour. And then what?

I die, Florent remains overseas, and I never see Lena again. I'm not even certain killing Saggy Throat will free my people, since many of the commoners sit by and watch when others fight for power. Yet I still climb the steps of the black stone castle, the overused soles of my boots nearly making me stumble and face-plant once more, but I steady myself. There's nobody at the gates of the Duke's Fort, and I see only two men where the bridge connects with the entrance. My dark brown eyes scan for the silhouettes of crossbowmen on the walls, but I see no one.

The scouts were telling the truth, then.

Suspicion never leaves me as the two guards don't even flinch at the sight of my weapons, although I wear the uniform of the Great General's councilors, so that's perhaps the reason they don't seem intimidated or wary. I clear my throat, eyeing both guards. Their visors are up, and they hold their spears with loose fingers.

"Lady Milagros Beausoleil," the one on the right greets me. "Great General Tarxi held the councilors' meeting three nights ago. You're late—"

"To the party," I finish for him, resisting the urge to either roll my eyes.

I hate it when they call me Milagros. It's Mila, and I'm not a lady. My brother should have become Lord Beausoleil, even if we don't share the same blood. He's older, wiser, and he's always wanted it. I don't want to be a part of all this.

And no, it's not a rebellious act. I believe in free will, and it doesn't matter to me if I'm Father's legitimate child. The title should pass on to someone who's capable and altruistic. I'm not that person. I'm not Florent. I came here because I hate General Tarxi's guts and because I'm sure the explosion that nearly killed me wasn't accidental, not because my heart throbs for the people of this smelly pit.

"I wish to speak with the Great General," I tell the other guard. "I know he's in here."

"Yes, he is," the one with the cringe-worthy jokes replies. "You know the way, but leave your weapons with us."

I offer him a nod and extend my left arm. The idiot reaches for it, and that's when I gather a lot of spit in my mouth and aim it at his eyes. It's gross and a little yellow, probably because of the smoking pipe and the herbs that kept me relaxed all afternoon, but it startles him, and that's when I ram the hilt of the sword in his nose before grabbing the weapon with two hands. I drive the pointy end into the other guard's mouth. ThenI unsheathe the smaller blade against the curve of my back to plant it in Sir Cringefest's eye.

I duck between their massive corpses, waiting for a volley of arrows or something, thinking that there must be archers hiding on the walls.

There aren't.

With the help of my heel, I push the guards' bodies while retracting my larger blade. I keep it in my left hand and sheathe the other. As I walk soundlessly past the entrance, my heartbeat fills my ears, and I can hear Florent's voice in my head. This is wrong; this is a trap. Security can't be this lax, and maybe this entire place is about to blow up. Maybe Tarxi isn't even here. It wouldn't take long for me to run back outside, to safety, but curiosity has the best of me, and I proceed down the endless hallway, where a black rug silences my every footstep.

The blood that trails down my Father's blade *drip, drip, drips* on the fabric. There's no one inside, and the throne room where the previous duke would hold his audiences is as humid as a mausoleum. They haven't lit a single candle, and the two statues at the sides of the black round throne merge with the rest of the dull background.

The councilors' meeting room is at the far end of this hall, with the wooden doors ajar. There's light on the other side, so someone is definitely inside the fort. Either that, or I'm about to witness some gore. Maybe my father's hanging upside down in that room, his throat sliced open or something nasty like that.

Come on, focus, Mila, I tell myself, flinging my long hair back when it tickles my neck. I'm wearing only padded leather, and yet, I feel weighed down. I stretch my left leg, pushing the wooden door open with my boot tip. I squint, and the room seems to be empty, but the part of me that's screaming in paranoia forces me to snatch a shield from the nearest empty armor set—I'm not even sure it's a real one; it could be a decorative shield, but I don't have the time to check—and I walk in.

There are two people in one corner, and one is General Tarxi. I can't get a good look at the other one.

"You've done an astounding work across the bay," he says. "I would have never guessed Quinten's location if it weren't for your many talents."

My jaw goes lax. Quinten is my father's name. I wait in silence, lowering the shield cautiously. They didn't hear me push the door open, or they're doing a great job at pretending they didn't. But what for?

"Ghostfort is yours," the other person—a woman— replies, and I drop the shield. It clutters loudly next to me, and Tarxi looks in my direction, his tiny black eyes connecting with mine. "I don't understand why you still sent everybody away," the woman continues, as though she didn't hear me.

"For this very moment," Tarxi answers with a broad smile, clapping his hands together and tugging at his lower lip with his pointer finger. "Come in, Mila," he adds in a chirpy voice, his partially bald head glistening under the dim light of the lonely chandelier. "I saw what you did to those two guards; I know you're here for me."

His words die as my stare travels to the woman who still hides in the dark. I let go of my heavier blade, but not before asking, "Where is my father?" My voice is tiny, and I don't sound like a twenty-eight-year-old woman. I sound like a child lost in the playing grounds.

"I don't know," Tarxi answers with a shrug, the gold embroidered in his deep green coat standing out as he takes a seat at the councilors' table. "I just know he's far enough not to be one of my concerns anymore."

Tarxi smirks, then beckons the woman forward. "Lena, please."

There isn't a part of my body that doesn't quiver in anger as she obeys him and steps into the light.

It is Lena. It's her golden eyes and her long, wavy brown locks. It's her freckles across her nose. It's her small hands fisting the black skirt she's wearing. I don't understand because she told me she was born and raised in the continent across the bay, and she even spoke with an accent when we met. But it's her, and the shame written all over her face is proof enough that this person isn't someone who simply looks like my Lena.

Bastards.

I am many things—brash, selfish, unforgiving... I never thought I'd be stupid, though. But I am because she hung out with me just to know where Quinten Beausoleil set off to after he and Tarxi assigned me that useless group mission of finding the totems of long-lost witchcraft only he believes in, and the last noble house of Ghostfort is no more, thanks to me.

"Mila," Lena whispers, stepping forward to stand behind Tarxi. "Your father was a traitor. I had to—"

"Is your name even Lena?" I interrupt her, caring very little about what she has to say. My father is scum, and I don't need her to tell me. It doesn't mean I wanted them to dispose of him, or whatever it is they did to him since he's missing. "Tell me."

She shakes her head.

"Why did you lure me in here?" I ask Tarxi instead.

"Lure you? You came in on your own accord."

"Because you sent my brother away and massacred everyone who wouldn't let you seize power after the Duke passed away," I bellow, my mind already at work to figure out how to kill them both.

I have the smoke powder to stun them for a bit, but this man's got a trick up his sleeve; I'm certain. Whether it's actual magic or guards disguised as furniture, I don't know, but he's far too calm to be an easy target.

General Tarxi chuckles, rubbing his wrinkled chin. "Fair point. I'll offer you what I've offered everyone else before you. Become one of my generals, and you'll remain the Lady of the Beausoleil family."

"Why?" I ask through gritted teeth, hating how the lying bitch behind him tries to meet my gaze.

"Because what you found across the salty waters will soon become a common interest for the surrounding kingdoms, and as a man who understands how dangerous magic is—"

I scoff then. Of course, he'd know.

"—I wouldn't want them to get their hands on those jewels."

"Why?" I ask, shrugging. "Don't you like a little competition in the conquest game?"

"This isn't about conquest," Tarxi states, the amusement gone from his voice. "Those artifacts could end our world. No one understood this, not even your father, and I thought he was a wise one. I do what I do for the interests of everyone who can't defend themselves."

I'm tempted to bite off the dead skin on my lower lip. But it would make me bleed, and the only blood I want to taste right now is Tarxi's, and that woman's. "I've never heard this much horseshit," I quip. I see them both tense at my words, and I wave my hands at them peacefully before I take another step forward. "But I'll give you the benefit of the doubt, General."

He arches a hairy eyebrow at that but stays silent. He stares at the pouch tied to my belt, and his lips curve up. "I wouldn't try that, if I were you."

"I won't, in fact."

I unsheathe my other swords, both of them pointing down as Tarxi and I exchange a knowing look—I'm not here to use them against him. Not now, at least. The old man relaxes back in his seat, ignoring Lena behind him, who tenses up. Her neck stiffens at the sight of the steel, and I'm tempted to smirk at that.

I let go of the shorter blade, Tarxi's eyes still fixed on my hands, and I maneuver the longer weapon with both hands. I keep my eyes on the Great General as a distraction meant for Lena, who screams his name as a warning, but I swing it and swing it fast—

Her head comes off with the next breath I let out, and it rolls on the iron table.

Blood lands on Tarxi's upper lip and licks it up.

I know he's hiding his stupor from me, even as his face remains relaxed. He's pulling at his fingertips. He didn't expect me to get rid of that lying whore so fast.

Neither did I.

The anger coupled with the excitement that his frightened look stirs inside me dissolves like snow on the first day of spring, and I take a better look at Lena. Her mouth remains forever stuck in that scream I silenced, and her glassy eyes stare at the ceiling. I follow that hollow stare, only to let my blade hit the ground. There are at least twenty archers strapped up there, aiming at my head and waiting for Tarxi's order.

Damn it.

The Great General laughs, his maniacal gargles irritating me to the point I wish I could deafen myself. I think I can kill him after all; he doesn't seem to have any magical trap all set up in this room, but the archers would take me down as well, and all of sudden…

I am afraid of dying.

I am not good at killing. I talk a good game, but I—

General Tarxi places a hand on my shoulder, and I smell the flowery scent of his perfume. Not the smell I pictured him using. Perhaps it's death that I'm smelling—in the South they say the scent of flowers is the scent of death.

"Do what your father couldn't do, Milagros," Tarxi offers me, and I can't help but watch his saggy throat bob with each word he speaks.

"It's Mila," I correct him.

"Mila." He pats my shoulder. "Bring me the heads of the four rulers of the continent, and I'll let your brother come back."

I want to spit at him the way I spat at the guard I killed, but I can't will myself to do it. I glance back at Lena's face, and my brow furrows.

I thought I had genuine feelings for her, but I feel nothing as I stare down at her. I didn't even ask if she truly did it or if she played a game of some sort, and the cruelty of my actions taste foul in the back of my throat.

What type of person am I? What if she was trying to survive or pretending to have done everything to help him but didn't?

"You're blackmailing me," I state.

"I see your potential, Mila." I hate the way my name sounds on this man's lips. It sounds like constant mockery. "You don't feel a lot of remorse, do you?"

I don't know if he's right. I know killing Lena was wrong, but is that truly the definition of remorse? Shouldn't there be something else?

"Then why wouldn't you kill the Queen of the South for me?" he asks. "On your way there, you might even find your father. Unless you wish to become Lady Beausoleil. I can do that too. It all comes down to who you want to be."

General Tarxi doesn't look like he's playing anymore. He gives me a serious look and folds his arms behind him, but not before nodding at the archers above. They lower their bows, and just like that, I'm no longer a target.

I hate this, I do, and yet, there's something dangerously attractive about the idea of killing more people to avoid letting them get to the items that Tarxi says are far more threatening than him.

"I don't want to be the Head of House Beausoleil," I answer him. "Father wanted me to be a soldier; my brother wanted me to be his advisor. I'm not meant for any of that. I want to be Mila and as long as I can be Mila, I will help you, General."

I could vomit in my mouth, but I need to be convincing.

I have to get out of here with my blades and both hands intact; I am not lying about who I want to be, but this man orchestrated a complete takeover and sent a wench to seduce me for information. I'm not about to trust him with the artifacts I'd found.

"You sail tomorrow," he tells me, turning his back.

Saggy Throat is pretty arrogant and confident. I could stab him right now, especially with his archers not aiming at my head anymore.

"But not alone, I hope you understand."

I freeze on the spot. I hear footsteps behind me, and the scraping of armor plates. I turn around and see another woman, another I know. Her dark brown hair is straight and not too long, her face square-shaped and her brow incredibly well-defined. Her nose is tall and straight, unlike mine, and her blue eyes compliment her fair complexion. She's tall and serious, a trained soldier and someone who obeys Tarxi like no one else does.

"Captain Petra Crellac will accompany you."

"You mean, watch me," I accuse him.

Tarxi smiles and nods at the captain of his guards. "This is as much of a test for you as it is for her. Petra disobeyed me once, and I must ensure she doesn't do it again if she wants to keep her position." He smacks his lips, the sound sending unpleasant shivers down my spine. "You sail tomorrow."

General Tarxi swaggers away with the elegance of a crippled elephant, and I hear the archers above fumbling with the ropes that kept them secured in place. Captain Petra is still stiff beside me, her eyes drifting to Lena's head, but she doesn't lose her composure.

I don't want to travel anywhere with a brainwashed foot soldier, but I've made my decision.

If I can't be brave in the face of death, then I truly am not Milagros Marcella Beausoleil.

Petra doesn't fully turn to face me, but she shifts her weight. "Where will you sleep tonight?" she asks.

"I'm not sleeping," I answer before I can even process her question.

"Me neither," she says. "Up for a drinking game at the Harbor Tavern?"

I don't like it, but the left side of my lips curve up. "Let's go, Pet."

"I'm sorry?"

"Do you prefer Tra?"

"I'm Crellac," she grunts, and I just stroll away, stopping before the doors when I spot the main rope that keeps all those archers in place fastened around one of the marble columns.

I unsheathe the longer blade at my back and swing it.

The archers fall on top of the iron table like a sack of rotten potatoes, and I suppress a laugh. Petra, or Crellac, grumbles a series of insults at my back, but I don't care.

This entire plan is torture, but I might as well enjoy it as much as I can.

Rainbow Wings

Sara Brunner

I don't know who I am, losing myself in this despair
Choking on my identity, losing consciousness without any air
My orientation caught in the gray zone, I'm neither here
nor there
Hiding in the shadows, shove down half of me
Bury it six feet deep, let it wither with the roses, let it be
But out of the dirt a new seed is born
Where love and acceptance, we will learn
For my heart bleeds just the same
Don't you see my soul is not a game
My love is just as deep
In my veins empathy will seep
I would lay my life down for the one I love
I'm not a sin to be disposed of
Under the the midnight sun
I will no longer run
Like a Phoenix I will rise
Grow my rainbow wings and soar into the skies

Little Red

Austin Slade Perry

This was previously published in Darkness Between and Deluxe Darkness

"Due to the recent string of animal attacks, authorities are requesting that citizens remain vigilant and avoid Cardinal Forest at this time," the newscaster warned. "Attempts to capture the animal responsi ble have been called off due to the storm expected to roll in later this evening."

I poured myself another cup of strong, black coffee. A misty rain had started to fall outside, casting a dark haze over the town of Willowbrooke. A full moon peeked through the clouds, illuminating the carmine treetops just north of the small coastal village.

"Does the sun ever shine here?" I asked.

"Roisin, my boy," my grandfather interjected from the kitchen, "In this town, we have four seasons: overcast, rain, snow, and mist. Now that you and your mom are living here, you're gonna have to get used to it."

I rolled my eyes, "Whatever you say, gramps."

Ding!

The front door opened, and frigid air swept over me as I zipped my red jacket up.

A rugged hunk with a dark beard and black aviator sunglasses stepped inside. He eyed the empty diner, fixing the collar of his fur-lined leather jacket, and proceeded to an empty booth.

I straightened up and walked over.

"Welcome to Granny Ruby's," I greeted. "What can I get you?"

He glanced up at me. I could feel his gaze pierce through the lenses and it sent a chill down my spine. He curled his lips into a slight smile. "Water," he growled, "and the rib-eye. *Extra* rare." I returned behind the counter, avoiding the customer's penetrating look. Normally, I wouldn't mind the attention from a handsome stranger, but this was different. I could feel it under my skin.

"Order up!"

I'd never seen a steak cook so fast, which was a relief. The sooner he had his food, the sooner he would leave. I forced a smile and set the plate down in front of him.

"Roisin, is it?" He studied me, taking note of my every detail.

"Yes, sir," I answered, averting my eyes from him. Theway he growled my name made my cheeks flush.

"Take a seat," he gestured to the empty spot across from him. "I'm sure your grandparents wouldn't mind."

His words caught me off guard. I opened my mouth to respond, but he raised his hand to stop me.

"It's a small town," he said, "people gossip, and I've got large ears." He chuckled, "Now, please, take a seat."

I had work to do, but something about him enticed me, so I slid into the opposite seat.

"It's not every day someone new comes to town," he said, digging into his steak. "What brings you here?"

My stomach churned as I watched the meaty liquid flow over his plate and into his fries. He picked up one especially bloody fry and bit into it.

"Just needed a change of scenery, is all," I explained.

"*Liar,*" he snickered, inhaling the air. "I've got a nose for bullshit." He leaned in and whispered, "No one comes here on a whim, so what's the deal, *Little Red*?"

I turned away from him, but I could still feel his eyes burning into me.

"Let me guess: nowhere else to go?" he remarked playfully. "Is Little Red lost in the woods?"

My fingers dug into the leather seat, "Maybe you should keep those 'large ears' out of other people's business."

The newscaster's shrill voice pulled my attention away from the man, "This just in, a new unidentified victim of a gruesome animal mauling has been found near Mountain Grove Hiking Trail. This is the third such attack in recent months."

That hiking trail was only two miles up the road from the diner.

"These attacks are getting closer to town," I muttered, swallowing down the panic in my voice.

The man took another large bite of his steak, the juice dripping down his chin. "A wolf has to eat."

"How do you know it's a wolf?"

"These woods are full of them," he explained, "Only a fool would dare wander out there alone."

A faint howl took my attention to the now wet and blurry window. The rain was falling faster. My eyes focused on the edge of the dark forest, where a set of glowing yellow eyes watched from the trees. I shuddered and looked back at the man.

"Is Little Red afraid of a big bad wolf?" he teased.

"No," I whispered.

"Don't lie to me," he leaned in again. His lips curled back into a wry smile. He lowered his glasses, exposing two bright yellow eyes. "I can see it in you."

I shook my head sheepishly, "Wh-wh-what are you?"

His grin widened, displaying blood-stained canines.

A crack of lightning flashed across the sky, illuminating the window just long enough to reveal the customer's reflection: a snarling lupine figure, baring jagged teeth. It was covered in matted fur, and its long claws scratched across the table.

I fell to the floor, striking my tailbone. Ignoring the pain, I scrambled across the linoleum to the counter, daring not to look back.

"Something wrong, Little Red?"

I glanced over as he finished his meal. He dabbed the edge of a smile with his napkin. His reflection shifted back.

I froze, searching for words stuck in my throat.

A loud crash broke through the diner. My attention shot to the kitchen, where my grandfather screamed, "Roisin!"

I found my feet and ran to him. A trail of bloody paw prints lead to the back door.

I stepped outside and saw my grandfather's body crumpled beneath the dumpster. His stomach was ripped open, and a pool of rain and blood formed around his body. He opened his mouth to speak, but his words were muted by gurgling blood.

Tears burned behind my eyes as I dialed 911. Another howl broke through the storm.

Ding!

The front door opened. I rushed into the kitchen and peered into the empty diner. All that remained of the mysterious guest was a large tip and a handwritten note on a napkin.

"See you soon, Little Red."

Not My Body

Stephanie Parry

How many times have
I wished for the flesh of my bones
to be different?

"You'll love your breasts when
you're married." my body does
not belong to me

They were like beacons
for others to touch and gawk
public property

Sneers, comments, and hands
that didn't belong to me—
there was no safety

Marriage did not bring
acceptance, while motherhood
allowed an escape

Pregnancy brought a
welcome relief with a new
purpose for my form

Death of gestation
forced me to face pain of my
foreign self again

So the lover comes, holding a mirror for my
soul-drawing me close

Fireworks collide, bodies clash and melt in one-
worship brings relief

"I love you," seductive words feel like home
for souls trapped in a foreign body

Shining light from the lover's touch
brings a painful recognition of truth

Escape looking-glass
love, find strength within to
survive on our own

Return when desire
for my lover's body does
not require loss

Heart of Her

Stephanie Parry

Eyes tell a story
of the person deep inside-
hidden from others

Work and care for all
Be the hero they believe,
Wear an aching smile

Surrender in the
welcome arms of a lover,
revealing the truth

Heart explodes as tears
fall, in the privacy of
soul crushing terror

Who am I? is asked
While the mirror reveals the
foreign body

Loathing the outer
exterior, betraying
the soft heart of HER.

Reborn

Stephanie Parry

Trapped inside a lie,
Covering pain with escape.
Keep it together

Wake up, work, go home
Go to bed, toss and turn and
repeat the cycle.

Is there some way to
Become real, like the rabbit
Of the velveteen?

Will love find a way
to release the truth or
push it all back down?

The breakdown arrives,
forcing truth to be reckoned,
Can I be reborn?

Disco Demolition Night

HRR Gorman

July 1979, Chicago

The bouncer at the Neon Hustle's entry smoked a fancy cigar outside the discotheque. The big, black man pointed down the neon-baked street. "Get outta here."

I lifted my chin despite my knocking knees. "You know about the ritual going down between the double headers at Comiskey Park. That little loser on the radio came up with a spell to help The Man steal your magic just as well as mine. You need me." I shook a cigarette out of my pack. A couple swift hand movements, and I lit the end. "I'm the coolest cat down at Hot Heels, and you can't say my magic won't help."

"Maybe you're as good as you say," the guard took a long drag of cigar smoke, "But none of 'em care. Ain't none of 'em want your fairy magic."

Just as he mentioned magic, the beat inside pumped louder. My feet itched, and the hair on my arms raised.

Magic infused the air, worked up by the combination of moving feet, beating hearts, and rhythmic music. "I get it. You've got your own spells here, and you and your bosses don't want me gaying them up. But none of your power, nor any of mine, will matter if we fail to stop The Man's ritual. Those square cats want to destroy disco and its magic, and they've figured out how to get it done. If we don't put things behind us, we'll both lose."

The man grunted appreciatively. "What you got that we don't already have?"

I released a pull, smoke emitting from my lips. "If nothing else, we got dancers. We got our own spells, too." I pointed into the club. "I can work something to this beat, if you want proof of my skills."

The bouncer nodded his head. "Alright. Then show me. You think we could use your fairy magic, give me somethin' right here."

I lifted a brow. "On the streets? Without any lights? No stage?"

"You beggin' me?" He pointed at the sidewalk. "Give me a fairy dance and prove you got the stuff."

I took a breath, smooth menthol lining my lungs. I'd hoped these cats hadn't forgotten back when I was in the closet, back when I danced at this disco. Still, perhaps forgotten was better than hated. After a final drag, I tossed the cigarette on the cement and ground out the flame with the toe of my platform shoe.

The music coming from the club was hot, heavy, and fast. I breathed in the beat and tapped my heels a couple times. I moved my shoulders up and down, then my feet grooved to the sound. A kick, a flourish of my newsboy hat, and a point to the ground. I waved the hat while my dance took me to the left, using the movement to grow my spell.

As the song ground to an end, I showed the bouncer the inside of my hat. "Won't be as good without a stage or lights, but... What do you think?"

A tiny storm of lightning filled my hat to the brim. He nodded, puffed his cigar. "Alright. You can come in." He sneered at me, lips shuffling the cigar to the other side of his mouth. "Call me LeRoy, if you have to talk."

So I followed LeRoy in.

The inside of the discotheque reeked of cigarette smoke and alcohol, much like Hot Heels. The club was nearly empty at this hour, and LeRoy led me between clean mahogany tables and the disco stage. Sparkling light bounced from the mirror ball turning on the ceiling. Brightly colored lights from the floor of the stage made the sweat on two dancers' faces sparkle. A woman's smooth dance shaped beads of water into a whip, and a man's robotic steps encouraged a chair to walk around behind him. The magic of disco allowed their dancing bodies to mold the world into something breathtaking, safe, gorgeous.

Their dancing and magic attracted me, but I followed LeRoy away from them. He puffed on his cigarette as he approached a large, circular table tucked in a black-lit corner of the club. Around this table sat an assortment of twelve men and women, each of them with a drink in hand and a cigarette in the mouth. Their faces glared up, suspicious.

"What's this?" a woman entangled with a peacock boa asked. Eyeshadow matching the blue in her boa caked her eyelids, and the right dance steps could harden her long nails into dangerous weapons. The lithe muscles in her arms told me she probably knew those steps and could boogie as well as—or better than—anyone else at the table.

LeRoy pushed me forward. "Got a little queer from Hot Heels. You know, the gay club down the way. Says he wants to help us stop Demolition Night."

I tried to ignore his slur and waved sheepishly.

"You test him?"

"Yeah. He checks out, Val."

I did a double take. I should have known—at least considered—that Val stood for Valerie.

"That guy on the radio wants to kill Disco Magic and take all the power my people have gained in the past few years. He's going to blow up a bunch of disco records and focus all the pent-up anger of some pathetic suburban honkeys on us. He wants to end our rise, end it forever." Val intertwined her dangerous fingers and set her chin on top of the little table she formed. "You think you can help us? And even if you can, why? You hang out with those crackers down at Hot Heels; can't they protect you?"

"Them? Protect me?" I scoffed. "In case you hadn't noticed, cops don't like gays, black or white. In any case, Hot Heels didn't prepare for The Man's treachery. We let Disco Demolition Night sneak up on us, thought there was no way the White Sox owner would let an anti-magic explosion go off in the middle of a double header. It's too late for us to create a defense, but we heard you'd got something." I leaned into the table. "We want in. We've got several dancers at high spell-casting level, and we're ready."

All eyes turned to Val, queen of this round table. Her fake lashes caught when she blinked. "High level dancers, huh? How many Flame to the Floor level you got?"

"Nine," I answered. This club seemed home to several of these highest quality dancers, perhaps even more than us.

She put her hands down to the table and leaned forward. "Desperate times call for desperate measures. I'm willing to entertain the idea of a collaboration, just for this emergency."

One man huffed and kicked at the table legs. A vicious cloud of smoke erupted from between his lips. "We ain't that desperate, Val."

Val tapped her long fingers on the tabletop, then said, "We'll teach your people the ritual. And Rollo, you're going to be right there helping."

The man who had kicked the table rolled his eyes, crossed his arms, and slid down in his chair.

"Meet us here, tomorrow, eight o'clock. Anyone who can't cut it gets ditched." She sipped a bit of a pink squirrel cocktail. "Now get out of here. We're not sharing all our secrets with you."

I nodded and backed away. "You won't regret this."

* * *

"How dare you?" Pale-skinned Robert put out his cigarette in the avocado-green ashtray, leaving the filter behind while the ashes smoldered. "You won't kiss me in public, but you'll march your ass up to some random, hostile club and as much as scream that you're gay. Hell, they could've been on drugs when you went over there—you could've been killed!"

I tried to ignore the racist undertones in his words and scooted my stool over. I held Robert close and pressed my chest up against his side. "These are desperate times. You know what happens if The Man wins! You know they've figured out how to exorcize magic from Chicago forever. You know what'll happen if we don't have magic."

Robert's tight pecs fell and rose beneath my hand with each breath. His gold medallion necklace was warm to my touch.

He cooed, "Yeah, but... but I'd rather have no magic than have no you."

"No magic might end up leading to death, for us at least." I squeezed Robert's hand. "You've heard about those guys who got sick in San Francisco. Magic's all they think's keeping them together. Doctors don't want to work on them, so science isn't going to help."

Robert rolled his eyes. "Okay. Fine. I can tell you're not going to listen to me tonight."

"You're already not listening to me!"

"I've been listening to you, but fine, I'll suck it up and—"

The sound of a window breaking interrupted Robert's apology and destroyed the solemn beat of the slow song. Another window broke, and men with baseball bats stormed in. Six entered, all of them big, burly, scary.

And one of them recognizable.

Rollo made his way over to my table, bat in one hand and glove covering the other. "How you feel 'bout tryin' to defile the Neon Hustle now?" Rollo grabbed me by the shirt collar and pulled me close. "I'm thinkin' bout breakin' your skinny legs, how that make you feel? Think you can dance up some fairy magic then?"

Robert squealed.

I pushed back at Rollo. "Do it. Do it, and your magic goes away too."

"Black magic ain't the same as fairy mag—"

"We all dance the same dance and access the same magic," I argued. "What I want, and what you should want, is to ally with us for just long enough to save the Magic. The white man—"

"Uh, *straight* white man," Robert interrupted, his face indignant.

I huffed. "The straight white man's figured out how to ban our Magic," I corrected. "If we don't stop that explosion at the double-header, all that unleashed fury will erect a barrier. All the Magic in Chicago will dissipate with a poof, like it never existed."

Rollo spat on the floor. "Better you don't have your Magic, then." He hit me in the legs with his bat, hard, just once. I fell to the ground, hugged my knees. Rollo held the bat above his head and blinked, blinked like he felt bad about beating a man while he was down.

He turned his attention to my cup on the table and hit the glass on top of mahogany. My whiskey splattered on the floor. Robert's cigarette butt in the ashtray rolled onto the ground.

"Take out their bar," Rollo said. He looked back down at me on the ground. "You stay away from my friends, y'hear? Don't want you gettin' your ungodly filth all over our discotheque."

The bartender held up his hands in surrender as Rollo's men came over to destroy his stock with their bats.

* * *

Val, a cigarette on the end of her long, thin holder, counted our number. "You told me you had nine. I gave up Rollo and Honey for nine of you, not seven."

"I know," I said. "I promised you nine Flame on the Floor dancers, but... well, Rollo paid us a visit last night. He scared two off."

"I know how Rollo and Honey dance. I can trust them. I don't know about your people." She gestured to my crowd with her cigarette, then replaced it on her lips to take a breath. "It's Monday. We have three days of practice until Disco Demolition Night. The ritual's complicated—if you can't cut it, we'll cut you. Understood?"

"Crystal clear," I answered.

Val reached into her long fur coat and withdrew a folded piece of paper. She dropped it onto the large circular table around which everyone—Hot Heels' people on one side, Neon Hustle's on the other—crowded about.

Val pointed to the document, displaying her plans for the ritual. "The music's a fast-paced, synthetic tune with natural voices, like "I Feel Love." We start the song tightly grouped, coupled male-female, understood?"

I nodded. It was their plan. At least Hot Heels was popular with lesbians, or we might have been screwed.

"Then, like The Man's anti-magic explosion, the dance itself bursts outward. We'll work on these grander movements today, memorize the overall effect of the song. We'll add footwork tomorrow, and by Wednesday we better be on point."

I nodded. "I get it. We push the explosion back in with our magic. It's... you figured out inverse fire magic."

Val nodded and folded the plans back up.

I gulped. "On to the dance floor?"

Val sighed, disgruntled. "Just don't make a mess of it. Those lights aren't cheap."

* * *

The sun stayed up late this deep into summer, making the 7:30 walk to Neon Hustle a lot less scary.

Robert put his hands in the pockets of his vest. His fingers curled around something, probably a lighter. "Man, maybe we shouldn't be doing this."

"Why not? We've already figured out this dance and spent a couple days practicing. We can pull this off if we don't give up. Just one more day." Nervous, I fingered my pack of cigarettes, wishing I could pull one out and light up. As I turned the last corner, a flashing red light caught my eye and I stopped in my tracks.

Robert ran into me when I stopped. "What're you doing, stopping like that?"

"Shit—it's The Man. They figured it out! They got the cops here."

Robert looked down the road to the shining lights. Several squad cars, red lights up and whirring, parked on the sidewalk just outside Neon Hustle. I couldn't tell from here if there were any arrests, but practice was going to be a bust. I took Robert's hand and pulled him toward the club. "Come on—we can't let this happen! We have to make sure they'll be alright—"

"What? No!" Robert smacked away my hand. "I've got a few tabs of LSD in my pocket. I'm not going down there, not with the cops swarming around."

My heart stopped along with my legs. "Bull," I said. "When have you ever done psychotropic drugs?" I huffed, held back a few tears, and made fists. "You called them, didn't you?"

"What?!"

"You called the cops! Thought you were getting back at that... that Rollo guy?" I pushed Robert away, then rubbed my nose. "You'll give up everything, everything, for that?"

"I didn't call the cops, man!"

"Then why lie about the LSD?"

Robert took his hand out of his pocket and pointed to the Neon Hustle. "What'd you think would happen if I go to a black disco way before opening time? You think those cops would just give us a slap on the wrist and say 'go home,' or you think they'd figure out some way to screw us? And look at you, you're double screwed."

I stammered, no words making their way through my brain to my tongue.

"Whatever." Robert waved me away and turned around, walking back to the bus station. "I ain't risking my neck out there."

"You telling everyone else to stay home?" I asked.

"Anyone I find, I guess. If Val's got enough people to keep practicing, they can come over to Hot Heels for a change. Get them to spend money on a bus ticket." He left, turning the corner and exiting my line of sight.

I held my fist. Sure, I could get in trouble—big trouble—but without Robert, I could do this. Val would know I hadn't called the cops. I took off jogging toward the Neon Hustle. I had to do it. Even if they couldn't practice tonight, we needed this collaboration to work.

When I reached just a few buildings away, some black-clad cops with their shiny shoes pulled a woman with long, sharp nails out of the building. I smiled at the few dribbles of raw, red blood trickling out of a cop's face, but that bubble of elation deflated when I realized what punishment now awaited Val.

I slowed to a halt. One after another, my new friends were dragged in cuffs out of the club and packed into a van like sardines. I shuffled to the side, into a small, dingy alley while the cops hauled them all out.

All of them. Each of the disco's Flames to the Floor dancers were excised from the club and loaded into a paddywagon.

I couldn't just stand here, useless, while these people were unfairly apprehended. If I hadn't gone and stuck my nose in their business, this might not be happening. I could be arrested if I interfered, which wouldn't end well for me, but... didn't they deserve my loyalty?

A strong, dark hand grabbed my shoulder right when I tried to leave the dank safety of the alley. I gasped and jumped, knocking the hand away before I got a good look at the face of the man who accosted me.

LeRoy... I shrank before his might.

"I-I'm sorry," I said, my voice faltering and squeaky. "I-I didn't mean for this to happen."

He took the cigar out of his mouth. "Do you know who done it? Why the cops are shuttin' us down?"

I shook my head. "I mean... I can't be sure. But even if I did know, I... I was the one who brought you into this mess. If it weren't for me trying to be the hero, none of this would've happened." I shrank further down the wall and involuntarily put my hands above my face. "I can't explain everything, but I'm the one at fault—oh, please, please don't kill me!"

The man took out a lighter and held the flame to his cigar. "I ain't gonna kill yo' fairy ass. Now stand up 'fore you piss yourself." He puffed a few times, getting the flame to bite into the tobacco.

I let my hands down. "You're not?"

"Nah. I think you've been on the up-and-up with us, even if your friends are a bunch of punk snitches. I know what Rollo and his crowd been doin' round at the Hot Heels. He didn't help much, even when we all knew we needed it. I'll let you in anytime." He put his lighter back in his pocket. "But I catch any of them fairy crackers within a mile of this place, your corpse gonna be harder to find 'n Jimmy Hoffa. Understand?"

I nodded and coughed. "I think I'm about to be sick."

LeRoy backed up. "Well, don't throw up 'round here. Get home first, and start comin' up with ways to fix this mess." He gave me a nod and a wink. "You're the one who brought us all together, and you're going to need to be the hero."

As he left and I let his words resonate within me, my heart rose.

There was still hope.

* * *

I took all the cash hidden in Robert's freezer and added it to the wad of my own savings.

"We're going," I said. "The record player's in the taxi outside, and we have about two hours before Disco Demolition Night starts."

He smacked my hand away. "They'll kill me, man."

"We could be killed anyway. I could be left to bleed out in the gutter, and I wouldn't be surprised if the cops looked the other way while 'just' a gay black man died. I wouldn't be surprised if one of them helped beat me in the first place." I pulled him up from the chair and to the door of his apartment. I tugged him down the rickety stairwell.

"Who else is coming?"

"No one. It's the last ditch effort." I pulled him out of the exit and to the cab waiting on the corner. "You screwed them over and sent them to jail. You don't have to admit it, 'cause I know. Now you're going to be a big damn hero and save disco magic."

We got into the back of the cab, driven by a guy who used to go to the church with me back when I was allowed. He gunned it when the door closed, and I held tight to the record player with the Donna Summer vinyl on top.

Robert huffed. The driver's cigarette smoke billowed out the window, so Robert turned the window crank just a bit and lit up his own. "That was my money."

"It was their club," I answered.

He breathed in a lungful of smoke, holding it a second before blowing it out his window, but didn't complain any further.

When we pulled up to the front of the precinct, the driver waved for us to get out.

"Help me with this thing," I told Robert, gesturing to the heavy player.

Robert helped heave the record player onto my forearms. He slid across the bench seat and took one side of the player, and the taxi driver sped off as soon as Robert kicked the door closed.

"No going back," I said.

He whimpered.

We carried the record player up the stairs and into the front door. Some cops exiting the precinct at the same time gave us dirty looks, but what else could be expected when two gay guys carried a not-quite-portable record player into a jail?

I put my back to a swinging door and pushed, then led Robert to a little window where a square, milky-white lady with horn-rimmed glasses wrote on a pad of paper. A small TV played the White Sox game behind her. Drunk suburbanites waited in the stands for the anti-disco intermission.

When we put the record player on her desk, she grimaced, deepening the wrinkles on her face. "What is this?"

"I've got bail for eleven people," I said. I pushed a list to her. "We need these people out, and we need them quick."

She blinked. "You know these people? Know what it means if you pay the bail?"

"I know!" I lied. I'd never posted bail before. "Get them and hurry."

She removed some paperwork, looked up some numbers, then counted through the cash. She returned a hundred bucks, then placed the rest in a safe nearby. She shoved a clipboard out through the small hole on her desk. "Go fill these out. When you're done, bring them to me and have a wait on the couches. Someone will bring them out shortly."

I placed my hands together in a praying motion. "Thank you," I said. "Thank you."

She grunted and continued doing her job.

Robert helped me move the record player to the couches. Other people waiting, whether for bail bonds or any other reason, stared at us as we placed the player on the floor. I looked behind curtains, behind furniture, until finally spotting an outlet where a reading lamp was plugged. I tapped the professorial-looking white guy reading a newspaper by the light and asked, "You mind if I take this?"

He lowered his glasses. "It's light enough outside."

I yanked out the light and put in my plug, then gave the thumbs up to Robert. He tested the machine while I filled out an insipid amount of paperwork. I placed as much information as I knew about myself and the people I was bailing out as I could, then made up a few items.

The lady at the desk accepted the documents, and the clock kept ticking. The TV behind her played the game. The pitcher kept pitching, the strikes and hits kept inching closer to the end of the first match.

At the end of the ninth inning, the players cleared the field and a truck pulled out an ominous box. Lined with dynamite and stuffed with precious records, the box whipped the crowd to a frenzy. The minutes ticked down, but the Neon Hustle dance crew still waited behind bars.

The lady behind the desk noticed me watching, so she turned up the volume. The shock-jock in charge of the anti-magic event took to his microphone. "This is now officially the world's largest anti-disco rally!" blared the TV.

The door just beside the desk smacked open just as the drunken crowd roared to life.

Val's eyes met mine.

Robert's hand held mine.

I willed my closeted past and my wide open future to meld, work together, even if just this once.

Now or never.

I nodded to Val. She waved her crew over. Robert lifted the arm of the record and started Donna Summer to spin.

The Man on the TV cajoled his rowdy followers. "Well listen—we took all the disco records that you brought tonight. We got 'em in a giant box, and we're gonna blow 'em up *reeeal* goood."

I couldn't let their ritual stop us now. "Hit it!" I called.

Robert let the arm down, and the electric tones with plastic beat lit into the air. I grabbed Robert's hand and took the first dance step.

Val grabbed her partner's hands, and the rest of the Neon Hustle dance crew fell into line. Our footwork led us into a circle, our breaths into sync. The blood in my veins rushed, like fire through my arms and legs. The black voice in the song contrasted with the unnatural instruments, all parts of soul, skill, love, and accuracy meshing together in harmony.

The man on the TV started a countdown.

At the end, when the fuses lit and the dynamite was supposed to go off, the bombs fizzled into smoke.

Disco records rained from the precinct's ceiling, pouring out all over the station. They piled up on the couches, the coffee table, and the record player that kept turning and spewing out "I Feel Love."

Unbelievers watched with mouths agape.

One asked, "How'd you do that!?"

When The Man on TV looked inside his evil box and saw it void of records, all my friends—old and new—closed in on me with open arms. No begging for forgiveness, no search for apologies, no fear, no blame.

"We did it!" they shouted, now unconcerned with whose skin they touched or how much love was transferred between them. "We did it! We saved Disco!"

The faces, arms, and lives around me reflected my past. Together, I hope, they spell a collective future. Disco Magic isn't just a work of dancing and singing: it's a work of hearts.

Today our hearts grew a few beats closer.

It's Snowing Again

Elizabeth Suggs

It was snowing on our mountain again. The flakes tickled my skin.

I had been climbing up before you found me. Ice crusted under my nail beds as frost ached my lungs. It was all too much, and I almost fell, but you grabbed me in time. I didn't even know you were there, but you'd been climbing that same path.

Somehow you'd seen me first.

Your fingers were also encased in ice; your nose hairs were made of tiny icicles. But when I kissed you, the frost melted. And when you touched my face, pushed past my frozen hair, my body became the spring's warmth, melting the snow where we stood, exposing the green grass beneath—the kind of grass you're not allergic to.

Now, we sit together on this patch of green, overlooking a winter that'll never freeze us again.

It's good to be warm at last.

Nameless

Avery Davis

Lyric's eyes flitted back and forth as they scrolled through the website for what must have been the fifth time in just a few days. They had never expected choosing their own name to be such a delicate task. Anything too masculine and people would wrongly assume they were a boy, and anything too feminine and people would mistake them for a girl.

Formerly, they had been far from concerned about what other people would assume about them. After all, such assumptions could be corrected and anyone who wouldn't make such accommodations wasn't worth dealing with in the first place. Unfortunately, it had grown to be an expanding weight upon their mental health as everyone they met thought them to adhere with one binary gender or the other.

They scrolled down the page, surveying a list of popular names as sunlight bloomed through their window. Was it morning already? *Aeden* blinked away the sleep from their eyes as they selected a new name from the list. Aeden was much more normal than their previous name; they could probably avoid having to deal with people viewing them as eccentric just for existing if they stuck with a name like that.

Aeden drew in a deep sigh and tugged at the collar of their flannel shirt. They briefly drew their eyes away from the screen in front of them to look at the twin-sized bed in the corner of the room longingly. If they could just pin down a name that truly captured who they were, they would finally be able to bring themself to sleep. After all, they'd come this far in staying up all night; they were determined to finally pick something out for certain.

Their gaze returned to the list of names, and Aeden became *Ink*. The name had a certain feeling to it that made Ink feel genuine. They parted their dry lips to try the name out, the name escaping their breath in a whisper. They could taste the humid morning air.

With a shake of their head, Ink decided the name wasn't quite right. It sounded just a bit too harsh to them, and while it seemed a stunning name, they felt it would belong better to someone else. So the search continued, and they clicked away from the website to find a new one.

Apple felt like a sweet name, and their lips curved into a faint smile as they imagined all of the puns they could make. No doctor would ever be able to come near them. Dad would probably be annoyed; he already kept asking them to just act like a normal person and Apple was certainly not a normal sounding name. The smile on Apple's lips faltered. *There was nothing wrong with the name, right?* People wouldn't view them as different or abnormal, would they?

They liked the name *Leaf*. Leaf had always been an individual who was in touch with nature, and it felt unique. Maybe it was strange. Maybe Leaf didn't care if it was strange.

Leaf was satisfied with their name for now. They were tired, and they liked it, so it would do at the very least until they had a good seven hours of sleep.

More creaking noises escaped Leaf's spinny chair as they stood up, their spine popping as they stretched. *Damn*, they must have been sitting there for at least five or six hours. They made a mental note to keep better track of time in the future, then collapsed on their bed and drifted to sleep before even a moment had passed.

Their dreams were filled with images of their life under countless different names. None of the names had really ever belonged to them. The one their parents had offered them at birth represented expectations of an individual that Leaf was not, and all of the ones that came after were never quite right.

Hours passed, and eventually, a knocking on their door stirred them from their sleep. A name that was long-since made unfamiliar to them resonated from the other side, and they groaned and moved to sit up. They still felt tired, though they were unsure if it was from a lack of sleep or fatigue from their namelessness. They called back to the door, "I'll be ready to go soon!"

As they disentangled their hair, they gazed into the mirror at their features. Their appearance had become something they were comfortable with, and suddenly, they found a new name: *Mirror*.

Mirror sighed and got dressed, a hoodie and jeans making for an outfit which would surely lead to them being scolded for informality. Not that it mattered, it wasn't a formal event, but their parents always got annoyed by Mirror's tendency toward more casual outfits. As they looked down to the gray hoodie they wore, Mirror became *Hood*. No wait—*Cloak*. There was much more of a dramatic flare to that, and Cloak had always had a bit of a dramatic side.

A hint of confidence blossomed inside of them as they adopted the name. It felt close. Still not quite there, but it was getting nearer to finding a name they really wanted. Cloak even felt that they wouldn't be overly concerned about people being cruel to them over such a name, they could deal with it if it meant finally being comfortable with themself.

Startled by the sudden realization that more than twenty minutes had passed since they awoke, Cloak turned to head downstairs. Their shoes clacked against the wooden stairs as they descended .

"Finally ready to go?" their mother's voice spoke from the doorway. She was unlocking the door, practically rushing outside as another name came to Cloak's mind. *Lock* was a nice name, and so they became that.

Lock stepped outside after their mother with an inquiry, "Where's Dad?"

"He's bringing the car over. Let's go, we're late."

Silently watching as the green vehicle pulled into the driveway, Lock observed their dad's expression behind the wheel. They then moved into the backseat as their mother took the passenger seat up front. Their dad said, "How are you doing, kid?"

Lock's eyes moved up to look at their dad. He'd been calling them "kid" a lot lately, but Lock didn't mind. It felt like an effort to avoid using the wrong name for them, and any effort to accept them for who they are meant the world to them.

They replied, "Tired." All of that sleep-deprivation was still lingering on them.

"We'll get you some caffeine on the way, okay?"

"That sounds divine."

In an only half-awake state, Lock gazed out of the foggy car window as the vehicle moved forward. The sun was still freshly in the morning sky, barely risen above the mountains. That probably meant they hadn't slept long, but an energy drink would help a lot with that.

Their parents spoke of something with one another in the front, but it sounded work-related and Lock was much too tired to be bothered deciphering it. The car passed by a field, and a tree standing in its center caught Lock's attention. What kind of tree was that, maple? *Maple* decided that was probably correct.

It wasn't all that different from being named Leaf, was it? A maple tree was much larger than a leaf, though, and it produced much sweetness. In truth, that didn't appeal to them quite as much as they thought it might.

All of this name-changing had them wondering, what even was a name? Was a name just something society labeled a person with to tell them apart from others? To a sleep-deprived mind, it seemed like such a silly concept. Everyone had a designated noise to get their attention and it was treated like a core part of who they were.

Maybe they didn't need to worry about this so much. They could just go by whatever felt right at any given time. That was no more peculiar than asking people to memorize a sequence of letters meant to convey who they were. No one could be defined by a name, not even if it were a thousand words long, and so what was even the point?

They smiled at their fogged reflection in the car window. Maybe there would be something that stuck with them eventually that somehow encapsulated all of who they were, but in truth, they had realized the only thing they wanted to be was *Them*.

Feels Right

Ashley Amber

She moves in closer
I freeze and think it's over
It will feel so right

Her lips remain soft
We kiss as the lift takes off
But mine are stale tonight

My hands find her waist
And her chapstick, I can taste
None of it feels right

We get to our floor
And I don't know anymore
None of it felt right

A long, hard goodbye
But all I can ask is why
Why it won't feel right

I think of the start
Of all those who stole my heart
No one stole the night

No want nor a need
And no desire ever seen
Not sure if it's right

Me, myself and I
So many more catch my eye
Do they all feel right?

I try to find a way
A new label or a name
Maybe this feels right

Waving through each place
Left me feeling pretty ace
Now it all feels right

Lullaby for a Lonely Sea

Elle Hartford

The Little Mermaid didn't marry the prince, but she is very far away.
And I didn't convince her to give up her voice.
But we did sing when she visited my cave.

The thing you have to know in order to understand this story is that it's bigger than it seems to be. People call her the "little" mermaid, and once she was that, it's true, but her story isn't just about her. The thing you must realize is that her father was weak. Yes, I know, he was king of the merfolk, and whatever other titles they've given him. But kings are just people. Everyone is weak at some time or another. So many people, be it on land or under the sea, seem content to stay that way.

And I don't mean weak in the physical sense. The King of the Merfolk could hurl a spear with the best of them—no one's debating that. But when it came to words, well, let's just say he was fighting with borrowed weapons. Each decree and demand he issued came not from his heart but from his advisors which whispered nonstop into his ears. He was king, but he had always been at their mercy. And that's the real shame of it, if you ask me. People say I associate with eels, but I'd rather have eels in the flesh than eels in disguise.

So the little princess grew up hearing speeches that someone else had said first, and learning only the songs that everyone already liked. Nothing ever changed in her world, and nothing was ever questioned unless, of course, those advisors were the ones doing the questioning. And then in her teens, she fell in love with a stranger in a storm. Well, wouldn't you? The poor girl never had anything in her life that wasn't vetted by half a dozen sycophants. Besides, teenagers have such an awful lot of emotion, too much for a rigid court to contain. Like kelp curling around the spires of the merfolks' palace, it was the most natural thing in the world.

And like that kelp, the love affair was doomed to die. Oh, not with curses and drowned ships and bloody seafoam, or anything like that. You really must set those things aside. I only mean what every matron knows: a great many loves will wither away. And in fact they ought to, because teenagers lack more sense than they know. Some lucky ones fall in love and are able to stick with it, I suppose, but the vast majority of them don't. Myself, I was just as starry-eyed as the Little Mermaid once. But that had been long ago, and I had to learn better, no matter how painful the lesson was. The truth is that stars are not sure signs of lasting love, and people are not dreams.

I knew this, but that is not what I told her.

What did I tell her, you wonder?

Well, mostly, I taught her a song.

* * *

She came cautiously to my cave, a place she had heard about in nightmares but had never laid waking eyes upon.

I made sure to keep well away from the glittering king-dom, but of course they always knew where to find me. No amount of deep water or forbidding rocks could keep out the truly determined. And she was determined, I'll give her that, but she was also obviously terrified.

I'd like to point out, though, that I wasn't the one to scare her. My garden is unruly, admittedly, but not what I'd have thought of as a ghastly fright. It is no manicured bed of coral, color-coordinated and pruned. As she came to my door, she floated above the garden like she'd never seen free kelp before.

I could see there would be much work to do.

Naturally, I invited her in. She didn't hesitate—didn't even look around at the decor. She had come with only one thing on her mind. We rested on carved rocks thousands of years old, I fed her oysters and wild jellies, and she told me how she loved him.

"I've never seen anyone like him," she said.

"Yes, dear," said I, "because you've never seen any-one new."

"I could feel an instant connection to him," she said.

"Of course, dear," said I, "you are new yourself."

She grew angry. "How can you say such things when I know that I love him? This is magic!"

And that's when I smiled. "No, dear, a storm and a prince is not magic. What you feel is the pull of the wave on the water before the tsunami. This is only the beginning of magic."

Well, it's hard to argue over the beginning of some-thing. For a moment there was silence in the water. She could have left me then, and found her own way to her prince on the shore. But she hesitated, and she tilted her head. Then she asked, "What do you mean?"

"Listen carefully," I told her, and I began to sing.

> *To yourself you must stay true,*
> *And this is the only thing you have to do;*

> *To your heart and mind be kind and true,*
> *And then great things will come to you.*

"That's not a real song." She frowned, as though only songs approved by the court and its king exist! I laughed, and she said further, "And it's very silly. You can't say you only have to be true to yourself when there's so many other things in the world to worry about. What about being nice to others? What about being with the one you love?"

I folded my arms. "What did I say to you?"

"You said… listen carefully," she guessed, losing interest. Her eyes slid to the door.

"Before that?"

She thought about it, but only because her years in court had made her obedient. "You said this is just the beginning of magic. But I already fell in love with him."

"I'm not talking about your love life," I told her, "I am talking about something much more than that. To your heart and mind be kind and true."

"I am kind," she pointed out quickly. "I saved him. Now I need your help. Couldn't you make it so that I can go on land and be with him? Give me legs, and a way to breathe air? This is true love. There must be a way."

I pursed my lips. Teenagers are very determined indeed.

"I'll tell you what I can do," I said at last. "I can show you how to make your voice so loud that anyone, even your half-drowned prince, can hear it."

"Okay," she said, clearly not satisfied with this answer except as a means to an end. "You mean you'll teach me magic?"

"What else have I been trying to do this entire time?" I said. But she took no notice. I decided to try it, to keep talking her through it. Maybe I could make life easier for her than it had been for me. And so I continued, "Very well. Start by closing your eyes."

"Right now? Okay!" She immediately complied.

I sighed. "Notice your hands, and your fins."

"Oh... kay."

"Notice your belly."

Her nose scrunched up. "Why am I doing this?"

"Because your voice doesn't come from your throat," I told her. "It comes from deep inside you. It speaks in everything that you do. So focus on your belly, and be quiet."

She almost spoke. But she did stay quiet. A look of strange uncertainty replaced the frustration on her face.

"Now focus on this question," I said very softly. "What is it that you want?"

"I want the prince," she said promptly.

"Uh-huh. What do you see yourself doing with him?"

"Well... being in love. And traveling everywhere!"

"So do those things," I whispered.

She opened her eyes, confused. "You mean I can? Just like that? He can hear me?"

"Can you hear yourself?" I answered. "Everything comes from the way you treat yourself. Saving others, being good, following your dreams, those things follow when you listen and understand your inner self."

"I already saved him," she reminded me. "So does that mean I can go?"

I hummed. "Did you save him? Or did you simply dive at an opportunity to exchange your life for his?"

She didn't say anything.

"Listen to that part of you. If you want to travel, then do it," I said. "If you want to love, then love yourself. When the time is right, love others—love anyone you want. And if you want to leave behind the court and its rules, you can. You don't need to find an excuse."

* * *

I hear all the news in the kingdom, eventually. It comes with the tides and the sighs of the whales, and I listen.

It seems she never went back to the shiny palace. But she never went up to the sandy shore, either. They speak of her now, the slimy advisors, and they say she lost her voice—they say she came to me and she gave it up, that I made her leave, made her turn on everything she knew.

Well, it is easy for them to say that. Easy to simmer the story down onto the shoulders of one familiar witch. Much easier to say I told her so, than to say that for years it was they who told her so. That for years, she had no voice to speak what she wanted. That's not a story they want to tell. It sounds too much like truth.

All I can say is that her voice changed.

And that she learned a new song.

To yourself you must stay true,
And this is the only thing you must do;
To your heart and mind be kind and true,
And see how great things come to you.

Magnificent Moth

Ericca Chavez

You were never a butterfly; you were never human. Always minding the rules of poise and purity. You fancied the shadowy depths of wickedness. Intimacy for a gothic palate became a forbidden freedom in a brilliant world of competition and judgment, disciplining those who couldn't outshine the rest. So, you put on the glimmer suit of linear humanity, dreaming that someday you'd meet the end of this undesired reality.

Embraced by an eccentric set you ablaze that night—an understanding for emotions you were taught not to succumb to suddenly ached in your veins. The flame you dreaded burned your flesh. Effortlessly unraveling a creature of the night.

You are a magnificent moth. Taking your wings, you flew for the first time without shame. Bygone is the limiting gaze of day, for you're free to roam the lovely night. Cupidity for your denied life grew, allowing yourself to bridge to other eccentrics. You become overwhelmed by this underworld of imperfect entities. The pliability of each individual: stinging, tender, and chaotic. You began to savor life differently, embodying a cross of Carmilla's and Lestat's sagacity for complex souls.

Elation for your revamp wasn't most notable by others, but by yourself. No more were you striking with ridiculous self-loathing; instead, admiring your own androgynous heart. Salubrious pride, the link your tormented self had always demanded.

You detested the light of altruism because it forbade you from your awakening, but you yielded that. Opting to love without restraints, to serve yourself and to exist openly. So relish your advent, queer soul.

Saturday Night Bacchanalia

Ronja Vieth

Waiting for
an apology, yet the monster

sits, this creature wrought
from pain of yours sports

your scars, contorts
your suicidal thoughts in her face;

The petals, stems of your bouquet
strewn like limbs she tore

apart, dismantling sutures
of the one too close. Sat

at my table you feasted, fury teeth
calmly sawing, ferociously

tearing those stitches you argued
had to be just so. Say,

where are my arms supposed to go,
ecstasy-marked, too marred to

to hug myself; where is
my face supposed to go,

gouged out lenses, lachrymose
lacks—your viewing glass;

where is my stomach
supposed to fall, lurched into

digestive juices leaking
through your teeth?

Render me a goat, expel
me from my pain.

My Medusa

Ronja Vieth

Stare at me and make me
Stay, I'll turn to dust

As fast as stone, caress
Your every lock, lay on

Your lids and lips that
Kissed so warm not long

Ago. Lay me down
And shatter me, scatter

My every sandy grain.
I'll curl around your feet,

Settle on every toe, make
Soft whenever you walk on me.

And if indeed I turn
To salt—you reminisce

Of sushi, soy, purse lips
To tongue so tentatively

The white and precious ore—
Maybe memory in—

Carcerated crystalline will
Draw a tear from you

And mingle with the salt of mine
To make me all but new.

Summer of Deceit

Trixie Bloom

In Memory of Trixie Bloom

Rory P. Harrison moved even more slowly than usual. The heat pushed down on him like the hand of God that had always been there. Rory was extremely uncomfortable. His large frame had fought bravely against the grueling ordeal of sightseeing. The battle had almost reached its climax, and he already had his eye on the nearest cafe table and suitable chair. He had begun to doubt his last-minute whimsical decision to travel to New York.

A few weeks earlier, tired of enduring his uneventful life, he had made a last-minute decision to see more of his homeland: America. Coming from windy Chicago, New York appeared to him to be the complete opposite kind of place. He'd never dreamed it would be so desperately hot here. His mind was moving much faster than his six-foot-eight inch bulk, which did not move so gracefully. He still stooped even after years of his mother nagging him to stand up straight.

As he sat down he felt wretched, repulsed by the sensation of his pale blue cotton shirt sticking to him. Rory hated anything that stuck to him. He could feel his thin blonde short hair sticking to his head with sweat. He regained his composure, just as he noticed a pretty woman approaching to take his order. She was dressed neatly in a checkered blue skirt, and pale pink crocheted top. She had a nice wide fresh-faced smile.

"Beer," Rory said. "Cold, please."

"Of course." She smiled, and then scuttled off quickly.

Rory was not a man prone to change, but he had treated himself by traveling on the Golden Express Train. He loved trains, and it had been an extravagant purchase, but for once, he was feeling indulgent.

He had nothing else to spend his money on anyway—only Johnson, his cat. He had no friends, no social life, no girlfriend, only nonjudgmental Johnson.

Once he was alone, he allowed himself to cross his legs, and felt the fat wobbling as he did so. He momentarily closed his eyes with discomfort. The umbrella gave him some relief from the sun, and as he sipped the fresh cold beer, his grievances left him. He listened to the New York accents, and viewed the skyscrapers surrounding him. The air was heavy and thick.

The streets began to fill rapidly, and people jostled to sit down under one of the pastel colored parasols. Rory felt almost human, and tried to smile to himself, if ever that were possible. He tried not to ruminate on the things he was compelled to conceal, life's cruel hand of fate that God had apparently handed him. He spent too many hours of his life trying to reason why, but was determined not to on this adventure. He looked down and a chocolate dog rushed toward him, as quickly as its little legs would allow. The dog was accompanied by a woman's anxious voice calling, "Fidelio, Fidelio!"

A dog man he was not, yet instinctively, Rory changed his life forever, in one heartbeat when he bent forward and scooped up the indignant yapping creature.

Following very shortly behind the dog came a swan-like woman, who glided towards him. Clearly, she was stricken, and furthermore, she was devastatingly attractive. Instantly, Rory wished he hadn't caught the dog. He held it out in front of him like a prize, and she scooped it from his grasp, kissing it frantically, gasping out thank-yous.

"Thank you, you're so kind!" She had a strange accent. She took his hand and kissed it gently.

Rory wanted to act like a gentleman, to stand up, but he also did not want to engulf her with his unusual height.

"Do you mind if I sit for a while with you under the shade?" she asked. Her Mona Lisa smile touched his heart.

His words felt strained as he replied, "Please do."

She placed the dog on the floor and her shiny, silk chestnut hair fell forward as she attached a leash to the animal's collar. Sitting up, she flicked back her hair and the sun danced on her curved swan's neck. Her appealing aroma reminded him of summer flowers. She blushed as she realized he was staring. A delicate light blue chiffon dress enhanced her tall willowy body, a style that had become all the rage in the seventies, overtaking the previously favored mini skirts. Rory hadn't liked sixties fashion, a world apart from this perfect vision of a woman in front of him.

She was a tall lady, maybe six feet. She had sparkling green eyes, almost exactly the same shade as his, only his were rounder. Hers were almond-shaped, and set off by pearls that hung around her neck and glinted from her porcelain skin.

The little dog lay down. A fancy rat, Rory mused, as a flawless hand was held out.

"I'm Miss Carlosa Reindl. I'm from Czechoslovakia. Pleased to meet you."

"Rory P. Harrison, Chicago," he replied, not knowing why on earth he was telling her where he was from.

Her perfect ruby lips smiled. "Well, Rory P. Harrison, from Chicago, let me buy you a beer for saving my baby." She motioned toward the dog.

Rory's mind started to race. It had been twenty years since he had been alone with a woman, especially one who wanted to engage socially with him. He shifted awkwardly. He didn't want to appear rude.

"Sure…" he said.

As they sat there, Rory noticed that Carlosa Reindl was painfully shy. Her beautiful eyes constantly scanned the floor. She reminded him of a very rare and delicate bird. He discovered, over three beers, and while Carlosa sipped her lemonade, that she was an antique dealer. She was here in New York to look for some new pieces.

"What an interesting profession!" he exclaimed. He was finding her easy to be with. A feeling he was not accustomed to.

Every movement she made was graceful. As she elegantly crossed her leg and sipped her drink, Rory was entranced. Stupid, stupid man, he thought, you can't go through any more. You know what she will think when she truly sees you… His inadequacies left him feeling sick again.

Rory began to feel very tired, which was a daily occurrence for him, as he couldn't stay awake like normal people. He tensed his eyelids in an effort to keep them open. I'm a darn silly man for having three beers… he thought.

Suddenly, Miss Reindl stood. He recalled that she had introduced herself as a miss. What man wouldn't sell everything to have her… Rory thought.

She proffered her hand, "Well, Rory, it has been a very enjoyable afternoon. I must be honest, this is not something I would normally do, but…" She held out a piece of paper. Rory took it, awkwardly, as she continued. "… Only, you seem different to me. A very kind, handsome man." Rory blushed. "You may call me while you're here if you need a tour guide; I know New York very well."

By the way she spoke so quietly, Rory could tell that like him, she was not used to this type of social interaction. He could only smile mutely as she sashayed away, the little dog skipping happily along beside her.

Rory walked slowly back to his hotel. The heat was a secondary concern now. His heart was fluttering, as unfamiliar thoughts floated through his head—She liked him… She liked him! HIM the freak, the mutant with genetic abnormalities.

He allowed himself to have fanciful ideas, glints of real contentment, and happiness right up until the moment he took his clothes off to bathe. The mirror seemed cruel as it accurately portrayed his ugly physique. He studied his tiny, tiny testicles, no bigger than grapes, that had never been held, accompanied by an unusually hairless body. Big pockets of fat enveloped his thighs, and his hormone starved breasts hung down comically. A man who cannot produce sperm, or make testosterone, who has women's physical traits. A man that cannot produce offspring. A man…

His thoughts made him laugh out loud at the taunting mirror. How many times had he been humiliated, bullied, mocked, beaten, and abandoned? He had promised himself a long time ago that he would never allow himself to become involved with a woman again. The pain would be too much to bear. He had consoled himself that his sex drive was, after all, non-existent, but he did miss having a companion.

"Useless!" he shouted at the mirror.

He could only partially get into the bath, as his whole body would not squeeze into the tiny tub. His thoughts were viciously self-deprecating.

Rory P. Harrison suffered with Klinefelter syndrome.

At fourteen, his testicles had remained very small, and he had never told anyone about that back then. Just as when his breasts started to develop. It was only when he had an accident during his late twenties that he'd confessed to the surgeon that he could not ejaculate, and about the other symptoms, before the diagnosis finally came back that he had Klinefelter syndrome, which meant he carried an extra X chromosome. The condition had rendered him very weak, thus he felt forced into taking a desk job in Chicago that he hated. He had happily withdrawn from society until now. He couldn't stop thinking about her.

Two days later, his fingers trembled as he dialed her number. She seemed happy to get his call, and they arranged to meet for a light lunch. "A real lady never goes to a dinner on a first date," she had told him.

He had purchased some flowers that smelled like her, and handed them to her as they met. Their height difference was minimal, and he managed to un-hunch for only the second time in his entire life. They chatted easily through lunch. Her laughter danced through the air and sounded to Rory like light musical notes. Carlosa was immaculate. Rory could not find one fault with her.

She leaned forward and touched his hand lightly. She was acting very coyly, an unusual quality in a woman during the open and sexual seventies. Rory did not like the promiscuity he saw around him at that time. Because of his low sexual appetite, he would often panic when the petting got intense. The more he saw someone, the more his apprehension grew. He pushed these thoughts to the back of his head, and enjoyed Carlosa Reindl's company.

His anxiety slowly diminished, as through date after date, Carlosa proved she did not care for fast sexual relations either. As she told him during their encounters over the weeks, it might be the seventies now, but they still had respectful and God-fearing ways in Czechoslovakia. He admired that about her, and was constantly surprised at how much of a true female she was.

He wasn't in any rush, in fact they hadn't even kissed yet. He wanted to spend the summer with her, and he had lots of holiday time owed.

"I can't believe you are only forty-two," she teased. Rory had told her he thought she was thirty-five, at which she'd flicked back her luscious hair, and giggled lightly. He found out she was actually forty years old. She had worked as a small child on errands to collect money to buy books, in order to learn English. It turned out by chance that she had a very good eye for expensive antiques, and she started to earn more and more money. People hired her to purchase antiques, often sending her over to the States. Her visa only allowed her two months here at a time. She only had her dog, and not one human friend. She said she preferred her own company, and was normally painfully shy.

Rory admired her in every way. He started to fantasize seeing her with their children, then the bad thoughts came crashing through, as he remembered that he would never be able to be a father. What woman would want that? Especially Carlosa, but then he could never recall her saying she wanted children, not even one reference. He decided against terminating their special meetings, which over the next two months became frequent.

She told him she loved to hear him talk, and she told him she felt safe and protected by his large size. She allowed him to walk slowly, and pause when he was tired. She never questioned why.

On walks, and historical visits, during theater shows, and meals out, their friendship bloomed. Strolling arm in arm and conversing on different subjects, time slipped casually by.

He began to think he could tell her. Rory began to think he was in love with Carlosa Reindl. He had never felt so confident, so tall, or felt this hunger satiated within him. A lion began to stir and roar inside him. Rory began to think it was fate that had brought him here. Destiny had directed him to New York. God had guided her to him. She was the love of his life. Time had made him even more sure of that, and now, on their most recent date, he had kissed her on the lips. Carlosa had not pulled away. It was a delicate snowdrop kiss that had lasted for seconds, and was burned indelibly into Rory's mind.

That's when he decided he would tell her the truth.

* * *

He had arranged an evening dinner in Times Square. She only had four nights left till her visa ran out, and she'd have to return to her own country. Tonight was the night he was going to tell her, but as she came toward him in her emerald green dress, Rory lost his courage.

What if she hates me? his mind interrupted, and a sharp pain Rory didn't welcome entered his heart. Yes! He realized he did love her, and wanted to be with her more than he wanted life itself. No, he couldn't risk it. He would love her as long as he could go on undiscovered.

She kissed his cheek. "Rory."

He really loved her accent. It was smooth as velvet. She soothed him and lifted him up. She already had his soul, his heart, and his love. He scoffed to himself that he would sacrifice the truth for Carlosa. He did not care if he was sick ten times a day. Putting up with the pain of not having her in his life was a far worse prospect.

Instead he had a different idea. He would spend every penny to return with her to Czechoslovakia.

"I must admit, I did wonder why it was such a fancy night," Carlosa said as she sipped her wine.

"Well it's not every day a guy asks a gal if he can come with her," Rory stammered.

She smiled coyly. "Yes, I must admit it would be quite serious. I want to say that I am a very private person, Rory. I intend to maybe never give myself to a man. How would you feel about that?"

His heart sang for joy. "That is not the least bit important to me. I enjoy your company immensely, and would like to continue to be in your company as long as possible."

Carlosa had agreed, and they began the arrangements.

"I do not wish you to pry, Rory, or push me. We all have our little secrets," she said.

Rory went quiet. What did she mean by that? Did she know something? Panic filled him. He made his excuses and left.

For the next two days all he could do was feel sick.

Reason battled with his ramblings. There was no way she could know… In his state of mental anxiety, he promised that he would tell her the truth while they were away. He convinced himself that he would, if only because he was unable to live with this constant torment.

When they met for lunch a few days later, they discussed the itinerary, and agreed on flying to Barcelona and then traveling by train across Europe to Czechoslovakia. It was particularly beautiful scenery, and slightly romantic, even though Miss Reindl was less bothered about this than Rory. He was convinced by now that she would accept him. She herself had said she may never want romantic liaisons. So why would it matter to her about his deformities?

Maybe she was a little secretive, but he didn't care. So was he. Her company mattered more than anything else.

They were due to meet at the station at ten a.m. Rory went to her apartment at eight that morning to pick up her luggage, but she wasn't there. She had a last-minute meeting with a client about a rare antique, and would meet him later.

He was excited. For the first time in his life he felt totally free. He imagined how it would feel after he told her the truth. He would surely soar to heaven, on her forgiveness and compassion.

Rory P. Harrison, started to whistle. Rory never whistled. Life was finally dealing him a winning card. It sure had been a long time coming.

For her he would be a dog person. For her he would be anything she wanted. He would take her to his home in Chicago and introduce her to Johnson, who would also love her.

Marry her—if that's what she wants… "Mrs. Harrison," it had a nice ring to it.

He picked up her suitcases, and inside her perfumed toiletry case he saw her passport.

He knew it wasn't very gentlemanly, but curiosity got the better of him. He opened up the back page, to find the photo. For a moment, time seemed to stand still. Shock filled every pore on his body. His eyes shifted back and forth from the name to the photo.

Romel Reindl

A very pretty man stared out at him from the photo. It definitely reminded him of Her.

He felt himself begin to faint.

* * *

Carlosa glanced at her watch. Rory was five minutes late. She hoped he wouldn't forget her evening bag...

Lo Lo's Lost Love

Jonathan Reddoch

Chloe found herself in a fog, both literally and mentally. She had spotted a beautiful fawn in the meadow, which darted off into a thicket at her approach. The half-deer half-woman shone like crystal through the quivering brown leaves.

The impetuous maiden was in the thick of it before she realized what she had done, following the creature into Deaf Leaf Forest.

"Lost, my love?" whispered a still small voice from a buzzberrie bush. It was the same dawn-sprinkled fawn. Her angelic voice froze Chloe in her tracks.

"Oh… I was looking for—" She was lost in those big doe eyes.

The fawn laughed. "Might we exchange names, my lovely pet? I am Lo Lo."

Chloe thought a moment and smirked. "My name is… Kytlyn… McGournet." She stifled a laugh at the little lie but was unable to conceal her severe adoration.

The fawn moved out of the bush, now transformed into a fully-unclothed human woman. Her natural form was perfection made flesh. Chloe found herself gravitating toward her.

"Oh, thank you for sharing your name. It is safe with me, my love." Sighing, she caressed Chloe's blushing cheek.

"My name?" Chloe chuckled, half-dazed. "Kytlyn's not my name. It's Chloe, but my friends call me Lo… Lo…"

Before she realized what had happened, Chloe transformed into a senseless deer sprinting on all fours deeper into the woods, while her new doppelganger strutted into Tumblestük Village to take her place.

Beauty is Found Within

Teresa Beeding

Adam flipped through the pages of a tragic romance from among the dusty shelves of his personal library; he couldn't stop melancholy from clutching his heart. His mother was the only one that heeded her own advice; judgment never once clouded her expression, as she read such stories with a loving heart and an open mind. There were many that she had read, she assured him. All were fantastic, different in their own beautiful, marvelous ways. Wonderful stories. And she had wished to read so many more.

Luckily, Adam was an open book back then.

Queen Amelie had loved her son's story the most. She had confessed to suspecting the plot twist from the beginning—and was pleased to know she had been right. On nights when his father retired to his chambers early, Amelie would whisk Adam away to the garden for an evening stroll. Asking all about his tale, and why he had decided to wait so long to tell her.

"I… wasn't sure you would understand," Adam had sheepishly confessed.

"Nonsense, my dear," Amelie had shaken her head. Her smile only brightened. "You are my son. You have always been my son. Even the 'great author' Himself knew this." A giggle welled up from her chest. "I must say He did a terrible job of trying to throw me off the scent. It is difficult to hide secrets from the eyes of a mother. Frilly dresses and etiquette class never quite suited you anyway."

"So you approve, then?"

"I more than approve." Amelie had stopped beneath the rose-covered lattice arch leading out of the garden. She took him in with proud, honey-brown eyes; eyes full of compassion, and the beauty of acceptance. A relieved sigh expelled from Adam's chest.

"But what of father? What of the kingdom? What of… of my future?" He bit his lower lip. Wringing the skirts of the dress he was forced to hide beneath. "If I open my book for others, will I ever find love that is true?"

Queen Amelie's slender hands had slipped into his. They squeezed tight.

"Beauty is found within, my dearest Adam. The one who reads your story back to front, multiple times, who understands the subtlety of its message… that is where true love is to be found." She kissed his forehead, and with that, the story of his life truly began.

Adam turned another page, though his mind began to wander to the times after that night in the garden. Bent over ancient volumes found buried in the depths of the royal library, mother and son had searched day and night for a way to make him totally whole. To free him from the illusion he was trapped under. Eventually, Queen Amelie had discovered a solution: an enchantress, known throughout France for her shapeshifting magic. For helping others such as Adam. And so, on a balmy summer evening after King Phillipe had retired to his chambers, Amelie and Adam set out upon their journey for the tale's perfect ending.

They had found the enchantress at the outskirts of a provincial village, living in a hut built of straw and mud.

She was kind and welcoming, very beautiful—quite unlike the volumes had painted her to be. "I have felt your arrival for days," she declared happily, opening the door of her hut as wide as it would go. "Please, come inside. Share with me your story."

So Adam opened his pages, pouring them out to the enchantress. She listened intently, with the same compassionate gaze as his mother. The same understanding smile.

"I can grant you somewhat of the ending that you seek." She leaned forward, voice suddenly dropping. "However, as with all magical properties, this spell comes with the necessity for equal exchange. What is given must be returned." Her green eyes shimmered. "What is it that you can offer me, young prince? In exchange for your story to advance?"

Adam shrugged, spreading his hands. "I can offer you money from the kingdom's coffers, or perhaps a precious necklace... I'm not certain what else would be of equal value for so great a spell."

The enchantress smiled. Her eyes turned to Queen Amelie, where they lingered for a long, silent moment. A contemplative moment. "Why not take your mother's advice to heart? That you shall never judge a book by its cover, no matter how much you may be judged in turn. For one of those books will be the one that pairs with your own— the complete ending to your story."

Adam nodded. "I promise."

The enchantress clapped her hands once; the fire in the hearth flickered wildly. Her eyes glowed a bright, sulfurous green in the deep and sudden shadow. Adam rose from the earthen floor, swallowed by comforting, warm light that streamed from the enchantress's fingertips. His transformation was swift and painless—fulfilling. Taffeta and lace disappeared, melting into sturdy cotton and wool. Heels became riding boots. Flaming curls receded. As his feet touched the ground, Adam ran to his mother, kissing her tear-stained cheeks and pressing her head to a broad, flat chest. And when he spoke, his voice was authoritative and deep.

He was finally free.

"Mother… look at me! It is a miracle!" He turned to the enchantress. "How can I ever thank you, madame?"

The contemplative smile had returned to her face. She inclined her chin, watching him carefully.

"Just remember what your mother has taught you, Prince Adam. Never judge a book by its cover."

Queen Amelie and Adam returned to the castle just before sunrise, to find King Phillipe awake and searching for them. Adam had never intended to hide himself from his father once his decision had been made; even if he had tried, the enchantress's magic made it no longer possible. He had silently hoped that the king would come to understand. To read his book through, just as his mother had. To love him, as any parent should love their child.

But it was not to be.

They were met in the foyer by armed castle guards, who had been deployed by King Phillipe in his search. Adam was apprehended, accused of being the queen's secret lover. He was completely unrecognizable to his own father—as he had always been. But when realization finally dawned on the king, he went mad. Queen Amelie had pleaded to the long-dead spark of compassion within her husband, but it fell on deaf, unforgiving ears. She was torn from Adam's side, taken to the castle dungeon despite harrowing protests and screams. To be executed at dawn for the proverbial "murder" of her child.

"You're a monster!" Adam finally cried, wrenching himself free of his captors.

King Phillipe's expression turned to stone. "No—it is you who is the monster. Look at yourself. You've become a beast; a hideous, monstrous beast!"

"But I am still your child!" Adam sobbed. "Why can't you love me now, as you have before?"

The king sneered. "Who could possibly love a beast?" He turned his back on Adam, as he had done so many times before; but this time, it was for good. "Take *it* to the tower. I never wish to look upon its face again."

It had been years since that night; years since his father had died. And still the words haunted him. Many times, Adam had tried to look past his father's narrow-minded transgressions, his unwillingness to listen to Adam's story. Tried not to judge the book by its cover. And even though he had become the prince he was born to be, that unwillingness to learn followed him among his subjects in wary looks and whispered conjecture. It only made him bitter and jaded, heart as heavy as the tragic romance aloft in his hands. Adam sighed, snapping the book closed. Tossing it on the table and putting his face in his hands. Perhaps his father had been right all along.

Who could possibly learn to love a beast?

* * *

As Adam was returning from the library, there came a timid knock at the castle's front door. He stopped, leaning over the balustrade for a look below. The ancient, wizened footman answered the summons, taking a candelabra from the hall and pulling open the creaky door.

A young woman stood on the snowy stoop. She carried a wicker basket filled with snow-covered red roses—selling them at the market in town, no doubt. She shivered terribly against the cold.

"P-Please," she said softly, "my horse was spooked by howling wolves, and I cannot find him. I cannot make the journey back to the village by foot, either. May I please stay for the night?"

The footman shook his head. "The master does not allow visitors. I am sorry, mademoiselle." He began to shut the door.

"Wait, please! I will freeze! Have mercy!"

"I am sorry—"

She sounded so innocent, so terrified. Suddenly reminding Adam of himself, so long ago, standing in that very same spot with certain death also staring him in the face. Something now foreign stirred in Adam's chest—compassion. It was an impulse he abruptly lost control over.

"Stop."

The footman paused, turning his old neck to peer up at the prince. So, too, did the young woman. Adam descended the staircase, approaching the two of them. The bitter wind nipped at his cheeks as he stopped beside his servant. Assessing the young woman carefully.

"What is your business here?" he growled, crossing his arms.

The young woman shook her head, brushing a flurry of snow from her chestnut hair. Honey-brown eyes observed him closely. "As I said, my horse bolted at the sound of wolves. I live at the far end of the village, and I will not make it home alive in this weather if I walk." Her eyes turned pleading. "Please, I beg you. I need shelter."

Adam sneered. "This castle is not on the main path. It is obvious that your route here was deliberate; your story is likely a ruse." Anger began to overcome him. Bitter, deep-rooted anger. He spread his arms wide. "Have you come to stare at the 'beast,' is that it? Well, take a good look!"

The young woman looked confused. "What do you mean?" She gestured back toward the blizzard, which began to white out the evening sky. "I saw the castle spires from the main road. It was my only chance for safety; I had no idea it was even inhabited."

Adam narrowed his eyes. "If you live in the village, how can you not know of the castle? Of stories about me? About the 'beast?'"

Her eyes locked with his. Contemplative. Confused.

"But… I see no beast. I only see a man."

Adam stared. His arms fell back to his sides, scanning the young woman for any sign of deception. When he found none, it left him feeling empty and rotten. Unsure of himself.

"What is your name?"

"Belle."

"Fine. Belle." Adam turned on his heel. "You can stay, but only for the night. I will show you to the guest room."

"Oh, thank you, sir—thank you!"

Adam led her up the sweeping staircase. The two remained silent, for reasons of their own. But as they passed the open door of the cavernous library, a wondrous gasp gave him pause. He turned to find Belle gaping through the door, wide-eyed and intrigued.

"You have a library?" she gasped.

Adam shrugged. "Of course I do. What of it?"

She turned an excited expression on him. Her porcelain face glowed in the soft candlelight, pink lips half open in a smile. "Oh, I love reading books!"

"You do?"

Belle nodded happily. "Books of all kinds! Fairy tales, mystery, adventure, romance… there's never a dull story to be told."

Adam raised an eyebrow. "Even the old, dusty ones? With dog-eared pages and cracked spines?"

Belle's eyes began to sparkle, her smile to grow. "Those are the best stories of all. The covers of books can be deceiving—you should never judge them."

He frowned. The words of his mother, of the enchantress, spoken clear as day from the beautiful stranger was surely a sign. It had to be. After so many painful years of hiding himself away, wallowing in guilt and shame, only today had he reminisced on the brightness of his past. On the promise he made never to judge another, no matter how hard it may be.

And gazing now at Belle, an innocent girl eager to hear stories of all sorts, the fist clenching around that judgment began to loosen.

"Ah… yes, of course." He gestured to the library door. "If you wish, I can show you my collection before you turn in for the night."

Belle clasped her hands, the wicker basket of roses trembling against her elbow.

"That would be lovely, thank you!"

Over a fresh pot of chamomile tea—which was refilled twice—Adam and Belle spent most of the night in the library. As fat snowflakes tapped softly against the stained-glass window, they discussed books of every subject. Stories that enchanted them, made them angry, broke their hearts. Adam was impressed with the provincial girl's knowledge, and even more so with her enthusiasm for discovery. She wanted to know more, to read more. And she was quite a story teller herself.

She was an open book. Just like he once was.

Within the night, Adam had learned almost everything there was to know about his guest. Her father had died not so long ago, and she was forced to sell roses at the farmer's market to make ends meet. The villagers cast judgment upon her for trying to survive on her own, for being unmarried—and uninterested.

"I would never want to be married to someone I don't know," she had said over the rim of her teacup. "I cannot even fathom it. Getting to know someone, for everything they are, is one of the most rewarding experiences imaginable. Getting to indulge in a person's deepest desires and secrets, help them celebrate themselves and grow… is that not what true love is all about?"

Adam swallowed, nodding slowly. "I agree."

Belle set her teacup down in its saucer. "What about you? I've talked your ear off this entire time, sharing more than I've ever shared with a stranger before. What's your story?"

Adam finished his tea, setting it down. Looking away.

"You wouldn't want to know."

"Nonsense." Belle's hand fell across his; loving and soft. Understanding. "You live alone with servants in this big castle by yourself. Surely you have many fascinating stories to tell." He turned back to find a soft smile on her face. "I would love to hear them."

Nervous, Adam pulled his hand away.

"It's getting late."

Belle nodded slowly, retreating her hand. She stood, brushing the wrinkles from her skirt in silence. Adam stood with her, watching her. Feeling guilty for shutting down. However, when Belle looked back up, her smile remained.

"Of course. Thank you for the tea. And for allowing me to see your library."

Adam shrugged one shoulder. "You're welcome."

They left the library together, once again walking in silence toward the guest room. All the while, Adam tried not to look at Belle. Fearing that one look would undo the chains that bound his story closed. He had locked it away, never to be shared again – except if he ever happened to find the one the enchantress said would complete it. He tried not to grow hopeful of the possibility that walked beside him as he stopped at the guest room.

"Here is the guest room. Make yourself comfortable." As an afterthought, he added, "And...do not feel rushed to leave in the morning. The blizzard is sure to make travel unsafe for a few days."

Belle's brown eyes were gracious. "Thank you, Adam. Rest well." Her smile returned. "Perhaps one day, I will get the chance to hear your stories."

Adam pressed his lips together.

"Perhaps."

* * *

Days turned to weeks; Winter into Spring. That spark of hope began to flourish. Adam invited Belle to stay after learning of her story, and she became a permanent, bright fixture among the once dreary halls of the castle. Breathing fresh air into the stale dungeon it had become. They spent most of their time together, reading over tea and taking long, contemplative walks through the garden. In a way, it felt as though his mother had returned. Belle's kind smile and genteel manner was one and the same; as was her compassion. Her willingness to listen. To understand.

Over time, their conversations turned softer. Gazes became fond, touches lingering. The chains around Adam's heart began to loosen; the pages of his book yearned to be opened and read once again. He realized that he loved Belle, and did not want to lose her. Didn't want her to see him as a beast and flee. And yet, all the while, as he feared Belle's judgment, he realized that he was breaking the promise he had made to the enchantress—to his mother.

And so, on a cloudless night at the end of May, Adam pulled himself free from the chains. By firelight in the library, he took Belle's hands and pulled her close.

"Belle...I'd like to tell you my story now."

Belle looked hopeful. "There's a story you haven't told me yet?"

"Yes. It's a story I've been holding on to because I was afraid. It's one that has many yellowed pages, dog-ears and a cracked spine."

"Those are the best kind," Belle remarked softly, squeezing his hands.

Casting caution to the wind, Adam opened his book. He told Belle everything. She listened with patience and virtue, round eyes widening as she hung on his every word. Hands squeezing his tighter; pulling him closer. And at the very end, when Adam had finished, prepared himself for ridicule and disgust, he was met instead with tears.

Tears of fulfillment.

"What a beautiful, tragic story," Belle whispered.

"You aren't disgusted?" He asked carefully—hopefully. "You do not wish to leave, now that you know the truth about me?"

Belle shook her head. "Why would I ever leave some-one I love?"

"You...love me?"

"Yes, Adam. With all my heart."

"Truly? You love me? Even knowing now that part of me is physically not as I appear?" His heart began to pound. "Even knowing that...that I am a beast?"

Belle was silent for a long moment. Then, a smile spread her pink lips. A beautiful, loving, and understanding smile.

"I have never seen a beast, Adam. I have only ever seen a man."

Overcome with relief—true, deep relief that he had never felt before—Adam realized he had finally found the ending of his story. He pulled Belle into his arms, holding her tight. And sealing it with a kiss, just as it had begun, he finally shelved his dusty, well-worn tome. Forever reminded that the most beautiful of stories are found within the most unsuspecting of covers.

Bloody Mary

Chris Tattersall

She had never known a time without the desire many considered deviant. As an adult, she had come to terms with what she was and she was comfortable with that.

As the sun dipped beyond the city skyline and the moon showed itself in the reflection of the dark office blocks, it was time to rise and feed her craving. Time to live her life.

Dressed in black from head to toe with an occasional highlight of scarlet in her jewelry, her perfect makeup and lining of her cape—a flourish she couldn't help but wear.

She was ready for the night.

She walked the cold streets to her usual haunt. It had proven to be a productive place previously and there was no reason why tonight would be any different. As usual, she would target the drunk, the vulnerable.

An alpha male of extreme proportions, whose height was only equaled by his width and bad attitude, took a dislike to her and threw a verbal assault denigrating her statuesque stance and stern look. His attack was harsh with evil intent, and it hurt her a little but it was no stake through the heart.

Her attention turned to reducing him to a shell, draining him of his essence. He had no concept of the power she held.

She savoured the taste of the thick red fluid. She closed her eyes in ecstasy as the liquid passed her canines, hit her tongue, her throat, and then her stomach. This one was a little spicy... She was fulfilled, at least for now.

The remainder of the night was a little mundane. She identified another potential target, but his blood alcohol level was clearly heading too far towards alcohol being the senior partner so she ignored him, allowing his excesses to destroy him. Unfortunately, all further potential victims managed to evade her attention before she could get her teeth into them.

She made her way home before the sun's warming rays hit the city streets. She entered her home with minutes to spare, an attic space in what was once a cotton warehouse. Spacious with an air that it had a dark past.

Kicking her platform heels to the corner of the room, she waited and silently squealed as relief hit her tortured extremities. She pulled the false lashes off with little care, tossing them to the bedside table. Next, the wig and false breasts were discarded before she untucked her manhood. She was transformed—just in time to see the encroaching daylight through a gap between his thick window blind and bare brick wall, like an eclipse of the sun behind the moon. He loved eclipses.

His husband woke to find the love of his life standing before him, overt black and red eyeshadow smudged across his exhausted face and breath smelling of his favorite drink, and the name of his drag queen persona: Bloody Mary.

"Good show, darling?" enquired the husband.

"Yeah, it was okay. A few hecklers. One big-ass guy was really annoying but he stood no chance. Bless him."

Exhausted, he removed his makeup..

He passed the bathroom mirror, knowing that looking in it wouldn't achieve much. If he could see his reflection, it would show pale, smooth skin, killer teeth, and the trace of human blood in the corner of his mouth.

The night's successes had been scarce, and he remained hungry. His husband fell back into a light sleep exposing the clean, unadulterated neck he had fallen in love with years ago, the tempting neck he promised himself would remain that way.

He leaned in for an embrace.

Penanggalan Awakens

Natalya Monyok

Disclaimer: Graphic and disturbing content

Constance ran to the toilet. Fiery vomit exploded from her throat, coating the bowl in chunky sick. The stench of breakfast twisted her gut into a knot. She slumped against the wall, chest tight with anxiety, and pulled out her cellphone to check the time.

Half-past four. Mizn was due to arrive any minute.

In the mirror, Constance stared at herself. She splashed cold water upon her flushed skin and kneaded her fingers into the bags beneath her eyes. Brushed her teeth and reapplied red lipstick. Practiced her best *everything is fine, don't worry about me* smile. Then threw her greasy hair into a top bun. That'd have to do.

Constance went to the bay window in the bedroom to steal a view of the main road. She listened intently for any approaching traffic, but all was silent on Glenview Lane.

A dagger pierced her insides. She placed her hand over her swollen belly.

"Is someone hungry?"

The unborn baby kicked and kicked, harder than it ever had before. She doubled over, dug her nails into her skin as if she could reach through and make it stop.

"Calm down. It's almost time to eat."

She stumbled over to the bed and collapsed on the mattress. She clutched her stomach. Counted to one hundred to distract herself from its tantrum. She reassured herself that all would be well once Mizn arrived. He always knew just what to do.

When the doorbell chimed, she struggled to get to her feet as a flash migraine stabbed her skull. She groaned and called out, "Just a minute!"

Mizn stood on the other side of the door with his sister and mother. Their smiles dropped when they saw Constance.

Mizn set down his backpack. "What's going on?"

"I'm just feeling a bit sick today." She glanced pointedly at her stomach.

"This pain you feel, it is only natural." Mizn's sister stepped out from behind him. She bore a thick Malaysian accent, her English much more broken than her brother's. It was a unique sound—slightly Chinese, slightly Indian—with just a hint of a swinging dialect Constance couldn't place. "You are eight months in. Very natural, yes."

"How did you know?"

"Esah is a midwife back in Malaysia," Mizn's mother said. "I am Wisama. It is nice to meet you."

Constance tried to speak, but another sharp kick from the baby nearly undid her.

Esah put her hand upon Constance's stomach, closed her eyes, and whispered something she couldn't hear. The pain quickly faded away as though it had never been there at all.

"How did you do that?"

"A mind trick. You only *thought* I did something."

"Esah has the magic touch," Wisama said.

"Are you sure you're okay?" Mizn said.

"I feel fine, honestly."

"Great," Esah said, and her smile stretched wider.

Constance was too enraptured by Esah to look away. Her features struck an unholy contrast, every little beauty a contradiction to the grotesque—sharp, crooked teeth housed in a pretty pink mouth; long, greasy hair that lay against a slender waist; obsidian eyes contained by a vicious squint. Her allure did not appeal to conventional standards; rather, she magnified an attraction that pervaded mind, body, and soul.

Despite everything she'd ever learned about social etiquette, Constance reached out to touch her, but Esah simply took her hand and shook it; her olive skin was smooth like wax, it belonged to someone too ethereal to be real.

"I am happy to finally meet you, Constance."

A strange warmth bubbled up in Constance's chest, only to be broken by Mizn, who pulled her into a tight hug. He kissed her cheek and told her how much he missed her while he'd been in Malaysia. She hugged him back as two weeks' worth of yearning caught up to her. Yet as she spoke, her eyes slid back to Esah.

Esah wasn't smiling anymore.

* * *

"I tried my hand at making an authentic Malaysian dish. Hopefully I did okay," Constance said.

She almost dropped the casserole dish as she placed it at the center of the table. She prayed Mizn's family would approve of her marriage to him in three months.

Wisama clapped her hands together and let out a squeal of excitement. "Rendang! How thoughtful."

Esah nudged Mizn with her elbow. "Rendang was our favorite dinner growing up," she said.

"Was it?" Constance said, sitting across from them.

Esah stared at her and bit her bottom lip. "I cannot wait to taste it."

"Well," Constance cleared her throat, "you'll have to let me know if it's up to your standards."

"Even though my mother always did most of the cooking, it was my father who made the rendang," Mizn said as he served himself a heaping plate of the curry-like slop. He took a bite and moaned in approval. "He'd approve of you making it with lamb instead of beef or chicken."

Constance could relax a little now. "I'm glad you like it."

"If only *bapa* was here now," Esah said.

"No sad thoughts," Wisama said. "We are here to celebrate Mizn and his new family."

Mizn reached across the table to hold his mother's hand. "I am happy, ibu."

"America has been treating you well?"

He gazed at Constance. Sunlight flecked his brown eyes with gold. "Very well."

"That is all I want."

"I'd be lost without Constance. Coming here was the best decision I ever made." He pulled away to eat more. "To think I almost didn't go to that grocery store on the other side of town. I met the love of my life on a random Tuesday after work, tired and hungover."

"You remember the day?" Constance said.

"I remember everything, and I always will."

"I wish I had what you two have," Esah said, quietly, as though she were only talking to herself.

"Are you seeing anyone?" Constance said.

Esah took a long sip of wine, eyed her over the rim of the glass, red reflected in her irises. "My lifestyle does not allow for it."

Mizn scoffed. "And what lifestyle is that? Reading books all day?"

She took another sip. "This is delicious, Constance. You have good taste."

What followed was a dull conversation about wine—its origins, their favorite kinds, the fermentation process—but the entire time Constance's mind was elsewhere. She couldn't help but ponder the enigma of Esah, how every time she looked into her eyes, she was blinded by hidden truths beyond her comprehension. There was a primordial sapience in Esah's stare, an esoteric wisdom that beckoned to her, that begged her to ask what it all meant.

She feared she was crazy for thinking such thoughts.

* * *

A thick smog settled down upon Portland, its skyscrapers obscured in shadow.

Constance walked through the city. Her stomach twisted painfully with every step. The baby was furious today and kicked ferociously to attempt escape. There weren't many people who milled about, only a few stray homeless men that catcalled her from across the street.

She threw her hood up and walked faster. When she turned a corner, a spark of panic raced through her so violently she thought she might vomit. She leaned against a brick building and tried to catch her breath.

She was alone, but she couldn't shake the sudden feeling that someone watched her.

Just when she thought the baby had stopped, it kicked again, this time more forceful than before.

She was on the verge of tears. "Please stop."

She continued on her way, determined to make it to the grocery store before she became too ill to go.

By the time she arrived, her paranoia had grown so intense it felt like everyone around her could sense it. She rushed through the aisles without looking at what she threw into her cart. A cold, bitter dread took over her mind and rendered her little more than a frightened animal. A hidden presence stalked her like prey, two watchful eyes stuck to the back of her neck, disappearing only when she turned to look. Her skull thumped with rage and demanded she leave.

As she moved on to the next aisle, she caught sight of a flash of black hair. She pushed it out of her mind and hurried to the checkout line, desperate to get home and sleep off this strange bout of schizophrenia.

* * *

Wisama and Esah sat in the kitchen and drank wine. They set down their glasses when Constance walked in.

"You look upset," Wisama said. "What is wrong?"

Constance meant to laugh to play off her pain, but she winced instead. "Just feeling a bit sick. Where is Mizn?"

"He went to pick up a part for the broken washing machine," Esah said. When she brushed the hair away from her face, Constance caught the stench of vinegar.

"Is something cooking?"

Esah shook her head. "You should go take a nap, though, yes? We can handle dinner tonight."

"Are you sure?"

She smiled. Constance noticed her teeth were slightly pointed. "Positive."

Constance sighed as her paranoia melted away. She was just tired and sick—that was all. "I appreciate it. I left the groceries in the entryway."

Constance trudged to her bedroom and fell onto the mattress, too weary to even climb under the covers. She quickly fell into a deep slumber.

She became victim to absurd dreams that made little sense. A pale woman who climbed into a vat of vinegar. A ghastly beast with a forked tongue. Bloody intestines entangled in thorn bushes. An infant who cried for its mother, its stomach torn open, innards spilt into the crib.

From somewhere far away, as though underwater, Constance heard voices. Laughter—her fiancé's, to be exact. She longed to go to him but couldn't force her limbs to move.

The bedroom door opened, then closed, and she could no longer hear Mizn's voice. Perhaps he had come to join her.

"Mizn, I don't feel right. I might still be in a dream."

At the foot of the bed, the mattress dipped. Hands

parted her legs, then a soft, warm mouth kissed the space in between. Constance called out to Mizn, but received no response—only the frantic, animalistic gluttony of someone who didn't fear God.

She couldn't move to hold him, nor could she muster up the strength to reach out and run her fingers through his hair.

He ravaged her with an intensity he'd never exhibited before. A fire of passion built in her belly, rising over the hump of her unborn baby, coming to bloom in her chest. A caterwaul echoed from her womb, begging, begging to come out.

Something burst from her sex and poured down her thighs. The stench of rust filled the room and violated her airways. She strained her neck to find the source of her excruciating pain, but all she caught were blurry glimpses of a figure that wasn't Mizn. A flash of long, black hair that grazed her skin. Sharp, white teeth, stretched into a crazed smile. A long, pointed tongue that moved in and out, in and out, and lapped up a thick, red substance. Two eyes, darker than the void, wept with joy.

Then there was rapture.

Flames of desire, of fury, raced through Constance's body and culminated in the nerves between her legs. The pain in her stomach became a vague afterthought as the shadow revealed to her gratifications unknown.

Constance opened her mouth to scream, to release this ecstasy she feared might kill her, when a wet hand slapped her across the face hard enough that orbs darted in her vision.

As the bitter stench of vinegar assaulted her, her limbs went heavy, and when she closed her eyes, try as she might, she could not open them again.

* * *

Constance woke up the next morning to a violent migraine. Cautiously, she got out of bed, but her legs were so weak she nearly fell over. She called out for Mizn, but he was nowhere to be found.

When Constance closed the bathroom door behind her, memories of the previous night came to her in waves. She sank to the floor as ominous thoughts took over her terrified mind. Was it all just a fucked-up nightmare?

When she remembered all the blood, she pulled up her skirt, but there was nothing there. She rubbed her stomach, felt her baby kick gently, peacefully. All was well, even if it didn't feel that way.

Constance went to the mirror. Her skin was sallow, sunken in and pale beyond normalcy. Dark circles set her tired eyes far back in her skull. Her blonde hair was in wild knots, like she had thrashed around all night.

She brushed her hair and applied makeup to her face in the hopes it would diminish how sick she appeared. She went downstairs and tried not to look like she was in pain as she sat down at the dining table.

"There she is," Esah said from beside her. "You look better today."

Constance ignored her. "Mizn, did you come in our room last night?"

He looked confused as he shoveled a spoonful of scrambled eggs into his mouth. "Only to sleep."

"That's not what I—"

Constance lost her train of thought as the stench of vinegar attacked her.

"Does anyone else smell that?"

"Smell what?" Wisama said.

"*Vinegar.*" She grabbed her head and groaned. "Tell me you can."

"I don't smell anything," Mizn said.

"Are you okay?" Esah said. "You are acting strange."

Constance looked at her. "I'm fine."

But her blood thrummed in her veins as she thought about her orgasm from last night. She could practically smell it—that sickly-sweet aroma of cum that haunted her even in her sleep. Had there been any truth to what happened at all?

Esah smiled. All teeth. Constance remembered the long tongue that moved in and out, in and out.

When Constance stared into Esah's dark eyes, a bizarre connection forged between them. A dull pleasure throbbed between her legs and only grew faster the longer their eyes were connected. Constance longed to ask her the question that lingered in her mind: *"Had you come into the room last night?"* But before she could muster up the courage, the baby kicked angrily. Nausea hit her like a truck. She quickly excused herself from breakfast under the guise of having morning sickness and needing a nap, which was the truth, as far as she was concerned.

In bed, Constance passed out quickly, as if under a spell, and once she was well within the throes of her subconscious mind, nightmarish visions of the grotesque kind plagued her.

* * *

A hideous beast, mighty in stature and deformed in build, loomed over a beautiful, albeit frightened, woman. Its skin oozed a black pus that dripped onto her face. It whispered a strange incantation, its forked tongue producing a serpent hiss.

Under a compulsion, the woman turned around and walked over to a large vat of piss-colored liquid. When she slid off the lid, the foul stench of vinegar made her gag. Behind her, the beast still whispered.

When she entered the vat, the beast placed its huge, clawed hand on the top of her head and pushed her under. She struggled to break the surface, but it was much too strong. Soon, her body went limp and floated to the top.

The beast carried her out and laid her on the ground. It knelt over her and ran its hands over her wet body, gently as a lover might.

It leaned in to speak into her ear. Its greasy mane left behind a lard on her face. Her eyes shot open, and within them, a manic hunger danced.

The beast's speech was mangled and difficult to understand, but one word could be heard as clear as day.

Penanggalan.

The woman smiled, her teeth sharp, her long tongue reaching out to taste something which was not there.

She had been reborn.

* * *

The sun split Constance's skull. Squinting against its wrath, she slowly sat up in bed.

She noticed the dried blood on her legs, dark like rot. When she reached to feel it, a shooting pain ran up her arms. She pulled up her shirt sleeve and gasped. Pink and yellow sores marred her skin, the centers of which were characterized by hard, black lumps that radiated fire when touched.

The baby fought inside her, panicking to get out.

Constance roiled in disgust when she pulled up her shirt. Her stomach was covered in sores too. Some leaked an odorless, black pus, their centers popped open. She stared in utter bewilderment but couldn't fathom how this could happen so suddenly.

At the sound of footsteps climbing the stairs, her trance was broken. She sprinted to the closet, grabbed a jacket and sweatpants, then rushed to the bathroom to lock herself in before Mizn could see her.

"I came to check on you, honey," he said, just outside the door. "Are you okay?"

"I'm feeling much better. Just normal pregnancy stuff."

Constance wet a towel in the sink and scrubbed hard at her legs, trying to get all the blood off.

"Are you positive?"

"Yes, I'm fine."

A faint, pink stain was left behind on her thighs. But at least the blood was gone.

"Need me to get you anything?"

Constance slipped on sweatpants and a jacket. She buttoned it up so that it covered the black stains on her shirt.

"I think a walk would do me some good, honestly." She struggled to catch her breath. She closed her eyes and willed her heart to quit racing. "I need to run to the store to get some ingredients for tonight's dinner."

In reality, she needed to visit the pharmacy to find medicine. Because certainly this was all just a strange side effect of her pregnancy. Surely, the pharmacist would confirm that. There was no need to worry Mizn by showing him the sores.

"Weren't you just there?"

"I'm making something special tonight," she said, and felt a pang of guilt at her outright lie.

There was a moment of silence, but he seemed to believe her. "Just call me if you start to feel sick again, and I can pick you up."

And with that, he left.

Downstairs, Wisama and Esah sat on the couch by the entryway, engaged in a conversation in their native tongue. Constance wanted to duck out without them seeing her, but the stench of vinegar stopped her in her tracks. Her last nightmare rushed back all at once. The beast. The vat of vinegar. The beautiful woman who, although her face was cast in shadow, had looked familiar.

"Where are you going?" Esah said.

"The pharmacy a few blocks away."

She had meant to lie as she had with Mizn but found her tongue would not comply. A chill ran up her spine at Esah's penetrating stare, as if she prodded her mind for secrets.

"See you soon, Constance." Esah smiled at her before turning back to Wisama.

Constance struggled to keep calm as she raced out of the house, her mind overcome with a savage dreads.

She was ready to keel over by the time she reached the pharmacy. It was a small, family-owned business, and Mr. Perez immediately rushed over to help.

"Do you need me to call someone? It's Constance, right?"

Constance struggled to remain on her feet as she wiped the cold sweat from her forehead. She pushed back her hair and tried her best to smile at him.

"I came here for some prenatal vitamins, but I'm afraid this little one has other plans. Maybe it doesn't like the bacon I ate earlier." She patted her stomach, wincing when she accidentally irritated an open sore. "Where's your bathroom?"

He pointed to the back of the shoddy pharmacy, off towards the right. "Are you sure you don't need me to—"

"Thank you," Constance said, and she hurried on her way.

But once inside the grimy bathroom, she fell to the ground as a cold violence consumed her. Ice climbed her chest and clogged her throat until a freezing black pus spewed from her mouth, covering the tile floor and splattering the walls. There was no stench, which was somehow worse than if there was.

She remembered her nightmare, the black pus that oozed from the beast. She remembered what it whispered in its haunting rasp.

Penanggalan.

The baby thrashed inside her.

Constance was a fool to lie to Mizn. She needed him. She needed to get home.

At the back of the bathroom was an emergency exit which spilled out into a dark, empty alleyway. It seemed to stretch on for an eternity in both directions, and she didn't know which way to go.

A sudden, yet faint, *pop pop pop* sound burst in her ears. She threw off her jacket and, to her utter horror, saw that the sores on her arms were breaking open one by one. Strings of black pus ran down her sickly skin.

Constance dropped to her knees and sobbed. She would certainly die from this agony. She couldn't even gather the strength to pull out her phone.

Her baby screamed inside her. It wanted an escape.

A warm wetness trickled down her legs. When she reached inside her pants to check, her fingers came back red and sticky with clotted blood.

Before she could react, that unholy stench of vinegar violated her lungs, so potent she gasped for air.

All was quiet in the alleyway now, save for her rapid heartbeat.

A shadow bobbed up and down against the brick wall in the corner, its shape difficult to identify. It was somewhat circular, with what appeared to be lumpy ropes dangling from it. It reminded her of Uncle Ted, his limp head swaying back and forth, the noose around his neck, the spare rope in the corner of his room in case he messed up tying the first one.

The shadow approached steadily until its black mass covered the world in darkness.

What came into the light was a being bred from the darkest nightmares.

A head floated towards her, its skin pale as the moon, with bulging crimson eyes set far back into the skull like that of an anorexic. Its grisly neck dripped blood and black pus; pulsating, grotesque entrails dangled from it, a heart connected by a set of shrunken intestines, a pair of shriveled brown lungs, and slimy blood vessels that entangled with its straggly, black hair.

But that alone was not what made Constance freeze in terror. It was Esah's head that edged closer and closer to her. Esah bore the same cocksure smirk as she had the day they first met.

Constance needed to scream, to run, but she was paralyzed and unable to breathe.

"What am I, you ask?"

Esah's voice was garbled. Black pus leaked from her chapped mouth.

Constance knew she could read her mind. *Yes, what are you?*

To look at Esah was to witness God, and although

Constance was panic-stricken, she also felt great revere for this being whose existence she couldn't comprehend.

"You should know what I am. I have been told you saw my transformation in your dreams."

Constance remembered.

Penanggalan.

But what is that?

The baby thrashed inside her, though she barely noticed.

"The world knows me by many names. Eternal One. Night Reaper. Cradle Wraith. There are many more still."

Finally, Constance understood. *You want my baby.*

Esah drifted closer. Her entrails billowed in an unseen wind. "I am so hungry, Constance."

How are you even alive?

"This is my true form. I do not need my body anymore to survive, only to appear human."

Constance tried to scream, but her voice came out as a whiny rasp. Every time she opened her mouth, the vinegar stench seeped into her lungs and constricted her breath.

Why do you have to take my baby?

Esah gazed upon Constance's stomach, and her stare haunted. "He longs to escape. He has tried, but he is too weak. All he did was make you bleed."

Constance held her stomach and silently pleaded with her son to try again, to try again and again even if it meant her own death.

"It is too late, Constance."

Esah shut her eyes and chanted in her foreign tongue.

Flashes from the night when Constance was given a bloody consummation conjured in her mind.

"Do you see, human? When I sucked from the nectar between your thighs, I too fed upon his placenta, just enough to hold me off until I could consume him in his entirety. I cleaned it off after, so you wouldn't be the wiser. In doing so, I drained you both of your vitality. You cannot escape me. You cannot even try."

Constance couldn't move, not even to wiggle her fingers. She watched, helplessly, as Esah drifted to her, her mouth open in a deformed, hunger-crazed smile.

She hovered just inches above her now. Her entrails dripped residue on Constance's clothes.

"I am sorry, dear sister, but I am just so *hungry*."

Yellow fangs emerged from her mouth; black pus spit out as the sharp teeth pierced her thick gums.

Please don't.

Esah grinned. Her mouth stretched to beyond normal human limits, a dark cavern which sought only death. The whites of her eyes turned a malignant red, bisected by serpent-like slits where her pupils should have been.

When Esah plunged her teeth into Constance's stomach, a peculiar tranquility took over her mind and rendered all her thoughts placid and dull. It was through an ever-shifting curtain of darkness that she witnessed Esah steal her baby.

Esah ripped through her guts. Lapped up her blood like a thirsty canine. Held him up. His pale, scared eyes. His screams. A film of red, obscuring her vision. A terrifying crunch.

Then nothing at all.

Esah and her baby were gone.

Constance meant to cry, but what bubbled up in her throat instead was a laugh.

Soon, two hands cradled her face between rough palms. Then, a harsh voice.

Mr. Perez knelt beside her, horror written all over his face. "What happened to you?"

She didn't respond.

He slapped her, but she couldn't feel it. "What happened!"

And Constance could only but whisper when she said, "The penanggalan."

To Bee

Alex Child

I wish I were
A bumble bee
Cuz then I'd start
Catastrophes

I'd conquer homes
Leave none alive
Expand my reach
And grow my hive

I'd press the button
Big and red
And launch a nuke
Towards Ireland

I'd poison wells
From coast to coast
Thin the herd
The world engross

I'm just some guy
With a goatee
I'm not that smart
But as a bee

I'd conquer land
And become queen
Then force the world
To kiss my wings

My hands are tied
They're watching me
But no one would
Expect a bee

Charcoal and Chalk

Michaela Rae

He was charcoal and she was chalk,
She offered her light, a snowy mark.
He devoured it, shrouded in night,
Luminance gone, a change of light.

In the binary of charcoal and chalk,
Shadows loomed, blurring the walk.
Darkness consumed a light once beaming,
In this realm, brightness ceased streaming.

Trapped in a dance of somber and light,
She found herself in a deep plight.
Her essence drained, her spirit cleft,
Within the void that darkness left.

Amidst the gloom, a quiet plea,
A whispered hope to be set free.
She found her strength, her inner fire,
To swim out of the dark mire.

From shadows emerged a vision brave,
No longer bound by the normal crave.
Colors burst forth, life anew,
A spectrum wide, of vibrant hue.

Truth revealed, no longer confined,
Past the outline, a new design.
A heart unchained, embracing the call,
In unity, celebrating all.

From the chasm of dark and light,
She emerged, a phoenix in flight.
In her world, now richly spun,
She danced under a newfound sun.

In her palette, she found her voice,
In her rainbow, she made her choice.
No longer tethered to past afflictions,
Her past life, now a work of fiction.

Where once was monochrome, dimly lit,
Now colors in harmony, perfectly fit.
She weaves her narrative, free and strong,
In a world where all colors belong.

Author Bios

Alex Child

Writing has a unique power, and Alex Child is just smart enough to know that he's nowhere near smart enough to accurately describe it. Between working half as hard as he should and twice as hard as required at his day job, he continues pursuing that indescribable emotional swell from relating to a literary character and sharing their experiences. He hopes his story brings you even just a portion of that rush.

Ashley Amber

Ashley Amber is a writer, author and dancer with 15+ years of experience in all her fields. Ashley is best known for her self-published fantasy/romance novelettes The Flip Side of Sad *and* The Flip Side of Love, *and has worked as an entertainment writer for several websites including SoapHub, MJ's Big Blog and Collider. As a queer asexual author, Ashley loves writing for and about the LGBTQIA+ community. As a former pro ballroom dancer, when she's not writing, you can find Ashley posting dance videos featuring her own choreography and tutorials.*

Avery Davis
Avery (Ava) Davis is an author who was born, raised, and grew up in the city of Bountiful. She still lives there today, with her two dogs and a whole lot of cats. In her free time, she loves to travel to interesting places and has a longstanding love for Swiss chocolate. She writes most days and her first book, A Thief's Lies, is a medieval dark fantasy book containing both intrigue and action. You can contact Avery Davis or follow her at: Twitter - @AvaDavisWriter Tumblr - @FaeFoolery

Austin Slade Perry
As a child, Austin was always told he had an overactive imagination. When he grew up, that imagination transformed into storytelling and his passion for writing. He also finds joy in other creative outlets, such as drawing, event organizing, and supporting his friends with their artistic passions. Writing has always been an important part of his life, and this project reminded him that it is always important to find happiness in the things you enjoy doing.

Elizabeth Suggs
Elizabeth Suggs is co-owner of the indie publisher Collective Tales Publishing, owner of Editing Mee, and is the author of several stories, two of which were in a podcast and poetry journal. She is the president of two writing groups, one being part of the LUW. She's a book reviewer and popular bookstagramer. When she's not writing or reading, she's playing video/board games or traveling the world.

Jonathan Reddoch
*Jonathan Reddoch is co-owner of Collective Tales Publishing. He is a father, writer, editor, and publisher. He writes sci-fi, fantasy, romance, and especially horror. He has been working on his enormous sci-fi novel for over a decade and would like to finish it in this lifetime if possible. Find him on Instagram: @Allusions_of_Grandeur_*

Natalya Monyok
Natalya Monyok is an avid lover of all things horror, choosing to get lost within the madness instead of succumbing to the mundanities of the mortal world. She is currently seeking representation for her psychological horror novel, Mortal Minds. When she's not putting her characters into terrible situations, she's

been known to train Brazilian Jiu Jitsu relentlessly. She is a blue belt in the martial art and hopes to achieve her black belt and open up her own academy one day. She lives in the suburbs of Utah with her loyal dog Ares, close to both Salt Lake City and the beautiful mountains.

Ginevra Mancinelli

Ginevra Mancinelli was born in 1992 in Rome, Italy, to a Filipino mother and an Italian father. Growing up between France and Switzerland, she studied Literature, Foreign Languages and eventually graduated from Law school in Lausanne, Switzerland. Abandoning the idea of becoming a magistrate after witnessing the system's idleness in a case involving racial prejudice against a black student, Mancinelli spent two years rebuilding herself and chose to pursue her passion for writing. Mancinelli writes from her perspective particularly when it comes to mixed races, age gap, stepfamilies, bisexuality, eating disorders, and depression. Her books are own voice.

Sara Brunner

Sara Brunner is a writer with a love for the avant garde, gothic, mysterious, and darker side of life. Bleeding melancholia and longing nostalgia through onyx ink. None of this would've come to fruition without Anna. The only person in this life who means the world to her.

Stephanie Parry

Originally from California, Stephanie is a queer poet and writer for multiple online publications. Her works focus on love, sex, relationships and transitions of all kinds. When not writing, she can be found flying around the world, worshipping at the ocean, or meditating on a yoga mat. She is currently working on her first novel.

HRR Gorman

H.R.R. Gorman fashions dark stories by night and makes drugs by day as a pharmaceutical process engineer. He grew up in the Blue Ridge mountains of North Carolina and was the first person in his family to attend and graduate college. He obtained his bachelor's, master's, and PhD in chemical engineering and now has come back to North Carolina with his nuclear engineer husband and vicious attack-Pomeranian. In between processing pharmaceuticals and delving into fiction, Dr. Gorman likes play-

ing Dungeons and Dragons. You can find more of his writing in the Dark Divinations and Lethal Impact anthologies, at www. hrrgorman.wordpress.com, or on Twitter @hrrgorman.

Elle Hartford
Elle adores cozy mysteries, fairy tales, and above all, learning new things. As a historian and educator, she believes in the value of stories as a mirror for complicated realities. She currently lives in New Jersey with a grumpy tortoise and a three-legged cat. Find stories and more at ellehartford.com. And while you're there, sign up for Elle's newsletter to get bonus material, behind-the-scenes sneak peeks, and goofy jokes!

Ericca Chavez
Ericca Chavez is a writer based in Utah. She's been featured in Spillwords Press, Cajun Mutt Press and Timber Ghost Press. Inspired by horror, the supernatural and the paranormal; she creates short stories, poetry and even artwork centered around these dark topics. Though being a creative spirit, she also writes about her Mexican heritage, the environment, mental health and the occasional romance. When she's not writing or painting, she can be found tending to her plentiful garden, listening to great music, studying occultish/ mythological subjects and reading an enthralling book with a cup of tea. You can follow her at: www. instagram.com/ericca.thewriter

Trixie Bloom
Loulou Farquhar aka Trixie Bloom is an author, podcaster, artist, and comedian, known for her captivating storytelling and unique perspective. Bloom's work explores themes of identity, love, and the complexities of the human condition. She passed away suddenly in the early hours of 4th of May 2022 at the age of 55, at home in La Alpujarra, Andalucia, Spain. Sadly, she passed before a Collective Humanity *was published.*

Teresa Beeding
T.L. Beeding was born and raised in West Sacramento, California. She wears many hats; a cancer survivor, a mother, a writer, and a medical assistant. She is the author of They Come at Night and Other Horrors, and has had her work featured in several anthologies and magazines. When she is not writing, T.L. seeks misadventure with her boyfriend, daughter, and two cats at their

home in the Hudson Valley. More about her work and life can be found on her website, tlbeeding.com.

Chris Tattersall
Chris is a Health Service Research Manager and lives with his wife Hayley and Border Collie in Pembrokeshire, Wales, UK. He is a self-confessed flash fiction addict with some publication and competition success. A recent obsession of his being writing Novella-In-Flash. He also hosts his own lash fiction website: www.fusilliwriting.com

Michaela Rae
Michaela Rae is an emerging author with a rich background in English Literature and Multimedia Design from the University of Utah. Starting her journey at the Salt Lake Tribune, she honed her storytelling skills, later authoring grants and marketing materials for the nonprofit sector. Michaela excels at crafting compelling content, a skill she's now channeling into her debut novel, which navigates the complex themes of power imbalances and overcoming adversity. Residing in a historic bungalow in the heart of Salt Lake City, she enjoys spending time with her children, capturing pictures with her camera, and advocating for equity within her community.

Want more?

Check out our current and future anthologies at
www.CTPFiction.com